The Black [illegible]ass

BARBARA DEVLIN

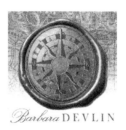

Barbara DEVLIN

Published by Barbara Devlin

The Pirates of the Coast Badge is a registered trademark ® of Barbara Devlin.

"Plaisir d'amour" by Jean-Paul-Égide Martini lyrics taken from the International Music Score Library Project (IMSLP), a virtual library of public domain music scores.

Cover art by Lewellen Designs

ISBN: 1-945576-90-1
ISBN-13: 978-1-945576-90-4

TITLES BY BARBARA DEVLIN

BRETHREN OF THE COAST
Enter the Brethren
My Lady, the Spy
The Most Unlikely Lady
One-Knight Stand
Captain of Her Heart
The Lucky One
Love with an Improper Stranger
To Catch a Fallen Spy

Loving Lieutenant Douglas: A Brethren of the Coast Novella

BRETHREN ORIGINS
Arucard
Demetrius

PIRATES OF THE COAST
The Black Morass

KATHRYN LE VEQUE'S KINDLE WORLD OF DE WOLFE PACK
Lone Wolfe

DEDICATION

This book is dedicated to my dear friend Captain KD Rowell of the Fort Worth Police Department. In so many ways, she is the big sister I never had, and much like the familial characters in my books, she is unfailing in her support and encouragement.

CONTENTS

AUTHOR'S NOTE

Gentle Reader,

While researching pirate culture for this book, I came across several scholarly articles that addressed the popular vernacular often associated with the genre and its larger than life buccaneers. To my surprise, I learned that most of the familiar clichés, such as 'shiver me timbers' and 'argh, matey,' derive from Robert Louis Stevenson's Treasure Island and Hollywood's exaggerated productions of Stevenson's book. In truth, the pedestrian colloquialisms have no basis in authenticity of the era. For that reason, I have omitted any reference to popular but disingenuous idioms. My decision should not be construed as a critique of Stevenson or other authors of the genre. Rather, I support an author's poetic license as an essential component of their voice. As such, my choice reflects my unique vision for my work, and I hope you enjoy my tale.

Thank you,
Barb Devlin

CHAPTER ONE

Atlantic Ocean
May, 1816

Virtue was a highly overrated characteristic in his estimation. In truth, he ranked it in the miserable depths of humanity comprised of respectability and righteousness. For the strong and fearless, the glorified traits of honor and integrity functioned as an impenetrable barrier to the excitement of the worldly existence filled with violence and debauchery in which he once reveled on a daily basis. In exchange for societal approval, grown men surrendered their dignity, and their whore's pipe, he would argue, to abide by a set of rules in which most had no say, and for what? High principles? Prestige? Indeed, such noble qualities sucked dry the marrow of life, leaving naught but the simple pleasures to enjoy, as the *Black Morass* rode the waves.

Sunshine glittered on the ocean, as a sea of precious diamonds, and a cool breeze sifted through his long black hair, as Jean Marc Cavalier directed the helmsman. Restless and yearning for stimulation, something to feed the hunger that gnawed at his harrowed soul, he approached with caution what appeared to be a burning schooner that he might offer aid, in accord with the pact he signed in a moment of weakness or perhaps insanity.

"No movement on deck, Cap'n." Tyne, the bosun, lowered his spyglass. "Should we continue our advance?"

"We will maintain course and heading, just to be sure there are no survivors in need of rescue." For some strange suspicion he could not quite shake, Jean Marc surmised all was not as it seemed, given the nearest vessel disappeared below the horizon before he could inquire after the circumstances of the misadventure. For a seaman, naught struck fear in the heart more than fire aboard ship, which could send an entire crew to Davy Jones's locker. And he had given his word to perform meritorious deeds for a full year, in trade for an unconditional pardon. At the end of twelve months, Jean Marc and his men would be free of past crimes, beholden to none.

But at what price had he bartered his autonomy?

It was for that reason Jean Marc refused to sail past the doomed lady. And then he spied activity at the stern rail, on the quarterdeck. "Come about."

"What is it?" Peering over his shoulder, Tyne narrowed his stare. "Is that a white flag?"

As they drew closer, Jean Marc smiled, and a familiar itch in his palms had him flexing his fingers. The lure of conquest burned bright in his loins, and he struggled with a craving for fresh meat, if only to reassert authority over his life. "It is a woman." He laughed. "And she waves her undergarments."

Perhaps fate smiled upon him, as the chit might be just the balm to ease his unrest and allow him to regain a measure of control. Obligated to the Crown, and no longer the master of his destiny, he thirsted for the power of ultimate domination, and nothing compared to the supremacy inherent in seduction.

"Bloody hell, she is a tasty bit o' fluff." Tyne licked his lips. "And a bottle of Jamaican rum says she is unspoiled, too."

"I believe you are correct in your assertion, *mon ami*." That tempered Jean Marc's ever-growing arousal, as he never claimed virgin's blood, because he preferred experienced whores who knew what he wanted and gave it to him, without complaint or inconvenient emotional attachments. Then he got a good look at the boon, in question, as the *Morass* glided to a halt, and full-blown lust threatened to consume him. Maybe it was time to sample the tender flesh of an innocent. "Ahoy, dear lady. Jean Marc Cavalier, most definitely at your service."

"Kind sir, I would be grateful for passage to Port Royal." Behind her, the masts collapsed, and she shrieked. How he ached to make her squeal with enthusiasm, as he would wager she could scream much louder with the right inducement. "As you can see, my current accommodation is about to sink, and I am in dire need of new transportation."

"Lower the plank." He signaled the crew. "As I am certain we can strike a mutually beneficial bargain." With a lush figure made for sin, and of that he could envision committing many with her, and alabaster skin he fully intended to explore in more intense inspection, once he got her alone, she presented a delightful distraction. "How is it your ship fell into such misfortune, and where is the crew?"

"They are dead." Tears pooled in her vivid blue eyes, and she emitted a soft sob, but he cared not for her sad tale. "We were attacked by pirates, and I hid in the captain's cabin, in a small compartment beneath a concealed floor panel, which he revealed he previously used for smuggling, thus I was spared."

"Come here, *Mon Chou.*" As the bow dipped below the surface of the water, he slipped an arm about her hips and whisked her aboard the *Morass.*

"Oh, do collect my bundles, as they hold irreplaceable personal items, including some of my mother's keepsakes." She pointed to two pillowcases, knotted at the opening. "Please, sir. I cannot lose them, and I shall ensure you are handsomely compensated, when I reach my destination, as I hail from a family of means."

"Is that so? Then your every wish is my command." And she would compensate him, all right, but not in the coin she proposed, as he had something else in mind for the delectable brown-haired wench. In seconds, Jean Marc jumped to the now high-pitched stern, grabbed the belongings, glanced into the waist of the doomed vessel, and discovered the remains of a massacre, which made no sense. At the very least, the sailors could have been sold into slavery, so why would anyone surrender such valuable cargo? A large crack in the boards indicated the ship yielded its last breath to the force of the ocean, and he took a running leap to safety. When he gained his footing, the woman flung herself at him and wept. "Now, now, none of that, *Mon Chou*."

Guileless and genteel, his unwitting prize had no idea of the scheme he would enact to reclaim a portion of his pride, as the King stipulated naught in regard to conquest of the fair sex. Indeed, she possessed no means of defense against his provocative persuasion, and he would employ everything at his disposal to well and thoroughly invade every inch of her. Before he landed the little angel on Jamaica's shore, he would instruct her in the art of pleasure, such that she would perform, at will, what even some professionals considered obscene, and render her quim raw. And then he would leave her, unharmed but a bit worn about the edges, without so much as a backward glance, as was his way.

"I thought I was going to die, and you saved me when all seemed lost." Well, he was not so sure he saved her, inasmuch as he delivered her from one precarious position to another, though she knew it not. Whimpering, she hugged him tight, and he savored her soft and feminine curves. "How can I ever thank you?"

Oh, he had plenty of suggestions. With a slight bend at the hips, she assessed her things, and he admired her round bottom. Then and there, he decided to first defile her arse and sail her windward passage, as he relished the compelling contradiction between the vulgar act and the pristine virgin, given she was no short-heeled lass or three-penny upright.

"You may start by telling me your name." Of course, buccaneer or not, Jean Marc required no such formalities to seize the treasure between her thighs, and he would feast on her honeypot soon enough, but he did not want to frighten her—at least, not yet, as fear could be quite provoking.

"Lady Madalene Davies, sir." An exemplar of perfection, her mouth posed an unparalleled enticement, and how he would engage her aristocratic, plump red lips about his stiff cock. Then she stared at the crew, released Jean Marc, and retreated a step. "Is this a passenger-for-hire ship or a privateer in His Majesty's Navy?"

"Not usually, and I am no longer a pirate." He advanced, as her chin quivered, and desire surged in his veins. "Thus I am willing to negotiate terms, if you are amenable." With a shrug, he trailed a finger along the gentle curve of her jaw. "Else I can return you to the sea."

"I beg your pardon?" Lady Madalene blinked. "You are *no longer* a pirate?" She made another perfunctory study of his men and gulped. "Am I in danger? Did you kill the *Trident* crew, and am I to suffer the same fate?"

"*Mon Chou*, you insult me, as I would have taken them captive were that my work. And never would I waste something so lovely." Swift and sure, he caught her in his arms, and she screamed, just as he claimed a lengthy kiss, to ribald hoots and hollers. When she wrenched free, pounded his chest with her fists, and prepared to protest, he nodded and thrust her into Tyne and Randall's waiting escort. "Take her to my cabin."

#

Freedom often commanded a steep price, in many instances exacted against the will of the innocent soul caught in its implacable lure, and Lady Madalene Davies pondered the cost her liberator, a self-proclaimed, one-time pirate blackguard who seemed much invested in his former trade, given his bawdy behavior and iniquitous demeanor, might demand in exchange for safe passage to Port Royal. But could she endure the consequences of such a bargain, as she foundered somewhere between the devil and the deep blue sea?

Out of place in her new cabin, which contrasted with her modest chamber aboard the *Trident*, she doffed her cloak and bonnet. A plush, red velvet counterpane covered the largest bunk she had ever seen, given Captain Hammond used a hammock, and the mattress hosted a mountain of matching pillows. The wall at the head boasted a salacious painting of a naked woman resting on her side, and its companion, a smaller work that featured a nude male and a female bent forward, pressed front to back, and engaged in some sort of odd activity, did little to inspire confidence, as she assessed her clean but well-worn accommodations and her precarious situation.

Behind the thick oak panel stood a surly

looking character she dared not challenge, and the small side chamber held naught but clothing. A locker marked with unique carvings revealed additional personal items, so she gave her attention to the hand-tooled desk, to search for some indication of the character of her erstwhile savior.

In the top drawer, she discovered a logbook, a set of maps and charts, and a deck of cards with the usual suits on one side and shocking images of ladies sans garments on the other, and she dropped the offensive items. Then her gaze lit upon a rolled parchment secured with an elegant ribbon. With a cursory check to ensure privacy, she untied the swath of silk, smoothed the paper, and examined what she realized was an official document, distinguished by its heading, *Letter of Marque and Reprisal.*

"Upon my word." Madalene gasped. "Jean Marc Cavalier *was* a pirate."

Before she could read the entire contents of the pact, a telltale voice brought her up short. Lightning quick, she restored the parchment to its secure space, glanced left and then right, and hugged herself. Adopting a relaxed stance, she peered beyond the window at the floating debris—all that remained of her ship, and considered her options, and of that there were few. It seemed she had traded one perilous predicament for another, and she knew not if she would survive to be reunited with her father, as her life depended upon a questionable creature Aunt Eileen would have no doubt described as a man with loose morals.

"You daydream, *Mon Chou*." Her not so chivalrous rescuer slammed shut the door, and she jumped. With a cocksure swagger, her less than noble knight strolled to the impressive desk, drew a bottle and two glasses from a drawer, and then pulled a chair from a small dining table. "Have a seat."

"Thank you." Stiffening her spine, she perched on the edge and settled her clasped hands in her lap to conceal her trembling, as she studied her opponent.

Unlike the sailors, the captain wore a white linen shirt, buckskin breeches, and a polished pair of Hessians. Chiseled lines comprised his classical profile but did little to dispel his menacing guise. A long, jagged scar traced from his left ear and across his clean-shaven cheek, disappearing under a black patch adorned with a large ruby, which concealed his eye, and a leather strip tamed his long ebony locks. Although he might have been handsome at one time, he struck her as a dangerous adversary, and she would zealously guard her virtue in his company.

Madalene cleared her throat. "Good sir, I—"

"First, let me correct you, *Mon Chou*, as I would have us understand each other." A sly smile played on his lips, as he leaned forward, and a tremor of dread traipsed her flesh. "I am no sir, and neither am I good. From this moment forth, you will address me as Jean Marc, as it is what I prefer, or I will give you to the sea."

"But that is not proper decorum for a lady of character, sir." Something in his expression, not to mention his threat, gave her a shiver, especially when he laughed. "And while I asked for transport to Port Royal, I would amend my request and have you put me ashore at the nearest dock."

"No, and I have no use for proper decorum." He shook his head, and her confidence plummeted to new depths. "You will tell me your history, and then we will negotiate compensation for my assistance."

"I do not have much money, sir—Jean Marc." When he arched a brow, Madalene gulped. "What I mean is I hold a trifle with which to pay my fare, but my father will reimburse you for any related expenses or a ransom, should you hold me prisoner."

"You sell yourself short, as you are a handsome wench, but I will clap you in irons, if it will make you feel better." Everything in his manner conveyed equal parts of power and peril, and she dared not protest, so she held her tongue. Tapping his chin, he narrowed his stare. "Everyone aboard this ship fills a need, and I wonder how you might serve me."

"What would you have of me?" Bereft of viable alternatives, she composed a list of skills, the sum of which she could provide to the captain's benefit. "I can cook a few dishes, and I can sew, but I am unaccustomed to manual labor. However, I am willing to learn, if you have the patience to teach me."

"Oh, I am more than willing to teach you what I require, and I hope, for your sake, you possess a strong constitution." His chuckle only increased her trepidation, as she had an inkling their intentions conflicted. "So you live well, Lady Madalene?" Reclining, Jean Marc gazed at her with unveiled interest and folded his arms, and she realized, too late, she made a grievous mistake. "Tell me of your wealthy father."

"In truth, I know little of him, as he departed Boston when I was but a child of four, and I have not seen him since." Never had her sire written a letter inquiring after her health, and her mother indicated he cared not for his daughter, but Madalene clung to faith, as she yearned for a relationship with her father. "When I was ten, my mother died of a nasty fever, and my grandfather became my guardian, but the task fell upon Aunt Eileen after he passed."

"And I presume Aunt Eileen is gone?" His eyes, so blue, reminded her of the crystal waters off Boston Harbor, and she would do well to avoid his captivating gaze, as it mesmerized her. "Have you no siblings?"

"No, I am an only child. And I lost my aunt in January, to an unknown malady." She bowed her head, as a tear coursed her cheek. "I was very close to my aunt, as she was all I had in the world, which is why I was so glad to receive my father's missive, asking me to journey to Port Royal."

"Why does he live in Jamaica, when he is an English lord?" The ex-buccaneer tapped his fingers to the tabletop. "Is he a wanted man?"

"Not that I know, but he is a stranger to me, in a sense." And that bothered her more than she was willing to admit to herself or anyone else, as she knew not what awaited her in the equally foreign place. "I suspect his request that I join him has something to do with Aunt Eileen's will. Given my mother preceded my grandfather in death, he left his vast estate, which includes a sugar plantation just outside Port Royal, to be divided between his surviving daughter and myself. As Eileen never married, there are no other beneficiaries."

"Am I to understand that, in light of your aunt's demise, you are the sole heir to the family fortune?" With an expression of surprise, Jean Marc stretched upright. "Indeed, you are the owner, according to American law."

"So it seems, per an attorney and a probate judge in the Boston courts." She nodded. "Now will you help me?"

"Were you traveling alone, and what precisely happened aboard the *Trident*?" The menacing captain rubbed his chin and shifted his weight. "Did the attackers take anything or anyone? Did you see them? If so, can you provide a description, as I am curious as to their identities?"

"My governess, Miss Wimple, accompanied me, but she was killed." In a flood of unpleasant memories, Madalene revisited the screams of horror, and she shuddered and wrenched to the present. "I heard plenty, and it was terrible, but I saw nothing, and for that I am grateful. Captain Hammond bade me hide before the pirates overtook our ship. Once silence fell on the vessel, I emerged from my makeshift shelter and found everyone murdered and the boat in flames. Had you not come along when you did, I would have drowned, as I cannot swim, which I already told you, so I thank you for sparing me that fate."

"Believe me, it is my pleasure, *Mon Chou.*" For a while, he simply studied her, and she fidgeted with nervous anxiety. "You had a governess." It was a statement, not a question. "How old are you?"

"Eight and ten," she murmured, as she toyed with the lace trim of her sleeve.

"Why are you not married?" When she shrugged, Jean Marc sighed. "Given your beauty and your inheritance, I gather you are popular in Boston."

"While I appreciate the compliment, I am not interested in such flattery." To her regret, she met his azure stare, which she suspected gleaned too much for her liking, and she swallowed hard, as he appeared on the verge of devouring her. "And I have no beau, given my father never negotiated a match."

"You would leave such things for your father to arrange?" He snickered. "The English treat the most important commitment a man and a woman can make as a financial agreement."

"If you intended to insult me, I take no offense, as I am an American." Madalene sniffed. "And my private affairs are no business of yours, sir."

"In that you are correct, and I told you that I prefer you address me as Jean Marc." He licked his lips, which she tried but failed to ignore. "Since you do not strike me as stupid, I can only presume you deliberately bait me, which is never wise, because I may take more than you are willing to give. Perhaps I should throw you and your private affairs into the sea." He snapped his fingers. "Then again, you cannot swim, so I encourage you to consider your words with caution, in the future, else you may not enjoy the consequences."

"I apologize." Never had she met anyone like Jean Marc Cavalier, and she wondered if the ocean might prove less dangerous. Still, if she hoped to reunite and reconcile with her father, she had to keep the irascible captain happy. Given her grandfather's cantankerous nature, she knew how to placate a temperamental man, as they shared much in common with spoiled children, so she had but to appease Jean Marc until they reached Port Royal. "To my shame, I spoke in haste, and I humbly ask that you forgive my inadvertent slight."

"You choke on those words." With a snort, he slapped his thigh. "Ah, but this crossing proves far more interesting with each passing minute."

"But I am sincere, Jean Marc. I do so covet compromise and will do my best to perform to your satisfaction, in whatever you command of me." Fearing a watery grave, she accepted the lone option at her disposal. She would defend her chastity, maintain what she could of her dignity, sacrifice her pride, pray no one ever discovered her ill-fated trip to Jamaica, and persist. With that, she resolved to indulge her unpredictable host beyond the usual social dictates. "Given you wish me to serve you, where should I begin?"

"You may pour me a drink." In that moment, he lowered his chin, scooted the bottle in her direction, and cast a half-grin, which she viewed as an olive branch, of sorts, until he whispered, "For now."

CHAPTER TWO

The sun sat below the yardarm, as Jean Marc leaned against the stern rail and admired his new cabin mate. No, they had not discussed her quarters, as he saved that particular joy for later, and he sincerely looked forward to what he anticipated would be a heated but restrained exchange.

A compelling mix of innocence, polite decorum, and fire, Lady Madalene conversed with members of the crew at the waist, without care, given she had no idea what naughty games he planned for her, but she would learn soon enough with whom she tangled. Rubbing the back of her neck, she shifted and peered over her shoulder. When she met his gaze, he smiled, and she dipped her chin.

"The lady is a kind soul, Cap'n." Tyne scratched his cheek and frowned. "She treats the men with respect."

"And your point would be—what?" Ah, the curve of her jaw presented a tempting confection he would trace with his tongue, and he would suckle and nibble her sweet flesh that night. "Have the tars completed the task?"

"Aye, but I do not like it, as she is young." The bosun shuffled his feet. "We could empty one of the storerooms, and create a private lodging for her. Say the word, and I will see to it."

"If I heeded your advice, how long do you think it would take before I had to kill a horny sea dog bent on sampling her honey?" Jean Marc snickered and descended the companion ladder, with Tyne bringing up the rear. "Now I will approve of the arrangements, ensure everything is as I commanded, and then you will send my guest to my cabin."

"We could post a guard—"

"No."

"Jean Marc, I know you are unhappy with the bargain you struck with the British, but she is a guileless babe." Tyne grabbed Jean Marc's arm. "Do not use her as a foil for your frustration, as you will never forgive yourself."

"I will do with her as I choose, which is none of your affair, and I have no conscience." Wrenching free, he turned on a heel and stomped into his domain. In the corner hung a small hammock, which had been strung unusually high and taut, to discourage Lady Madalene from using it. As he tugged on the stiff rope, he laughed. "Perfect. Now, bring her to me."

"Cap'n, please." With a huff, Tyne lingered in the doorway. "Will you not reconsider?"

"Do as I say." When Tyne folded his arms, Jean Marc narrowed his stare. "What is wrong, old friend? What is she to you?"

"In truth, nothing." The bosun furrowed his brow. "But she reminds me of Adele, God rest her, when we first married. And Lady Madalene is not your normal fare. She can be hurt." Tyne raked his fingers through his hair. "I have known you since you were a wee lad, when I sailed with your father, and we have committed some horrible deeds in our lifetime."

"So?" Jean Marc shrugged. "What of it?"

"Signing that pact was the smartest and

most selfless thing you have ever done, and I would hate to see you ruin it for a woman." Shaking his head, Tyne glanced at the floor. "Our time is ended, and either we change with the evolving world in which we live, or we cease to exist. Your sacrifice ensures the crew's future, and I am proud of you. Yet I know the decision came at a steep cost, as you pace the decks like a caged jungle cat. But Lady Madalene is blameless. Do not use her like some cheap brothel whore."

"I am only going to engage in a bit of sport, and then I will release her." Not for an instant did he suffer a twinge of reluctance. "And who knows, she might enjoy it." Then he bared his teeth. "Have the men bring in the tub, fill it with warm water, and then fetch the lady. And refrain from further criticism of my actions, for which I alone shall atone."

"Aye, Cap'n." Grumbling under his breath, Tyne slammed the oak panel behind him.

Two pillowcases perched on the table, and Jean Marc untied the knots at the openings. One bundle consisted of ladies garments, which he found rather mundane, but the other improvised sack held a collection of documents, some books, and several miniature portraits. An impressive leather journal caught his attention, and he flipped through the crisp pages, as the mates, carrying loaded and steaming buckets, fulfilled part of Jean Marc's orders.

Numerous entries detailed an estimable fortune, along with various properties, and he realized his passenger was, indeed, an heiress. For a scarce second, he mulled Tyne's protest and reappraised the situation. The prospect of seducing and corrupting a gentle creature of such wealth and prestige fueled an intense hunger impossible to resist. He had to have the exquisite Lady Madalene, and he counted the utter defilement of her virtue as a boon he would seize to quiet the turmoil raging in his veins, which he would claim without compunction.

"You summoned me, Jean Marc?" The soft, melodic tone of her American accent kissed his ears. "Have you a service for me to perform?"

Oh, yes.

"I do." Glancing at the hammock, he nodded. "Your accommodation is prepared."

"What?" As he expected, she shrieked. "You must be joking, as I cannot share a room with you. It is out of the question."

"You will sleep here, and you will show proper gratitude for my generosity." Doffing his boots, he smiled in anticipation of another outburst.

"But we are not married. It is undignified, and I will not do it." With clenched fists, she opened her mouth, peered at him, and compressed her lips. "What manner of man are you, to take advantage of a woman in distress?"

"One with little patience for mutiny, *Mon Chou*." In seconds, he unbuttoned and shed his shirt, and she averted her gaze. "If you would rather bunk with the crew, I grant permission."

"You call that an acceptable alternative?" She buried her face in her hands. "In either case, I shall be ruined."

"How so?" he inquired.

"When it becomes known that I shared a room with you, I will never find a husband." It was a rare sight to witness the death of naiveté, and he savored the moment, as she gave vent to a sob of despair and slumped forward. "It is bad enough that I journey without a chaperone."

"Come now, you act as if I just announced an intent to kill you." Never had he understood the female penchant for drama.

"But it is a death, of sorts." There was a certain beauty in her misery that reminded him of another time and place. "I wish to wed and build a family, but my shame will fill the scandal sheets and end all hope for a match. To know I will never achieve my dream breaks my heart."

"You do not think you overestimate the circumstances, given you were marooned, in a sense, and had no choice but to avail yourself of my hospitality? Or would it have been better had you gone down with the ship?" In that instant, she seemed preoccupied with his bare chest. "Do you believe my men and I mingle in polite society and spread gossip, as I can assure you we do not move in such circles?"

"No." When he unhooked his breeches, she met his stare. "What are you doing?"

"I am going to bathe." Quick as a flash, she turned toward the door, and he stripped off the last of his clothing. "And that is why I requested your attendance."

"Oh?" Stiffening her spine, she trembled. "But I am not sure what your personal habits have to do with me."

"You will scrub my back." A bar of soap and a sponge rested on the washstand, and Jean Marc retrieved the items before sinking beneath the water. "We have an agreement, and I hold you to it, Maddie. Whether or not you prefer it, we struck an honest bargain, and you will serve me." The pet name came to him as if from nowhere, and he braced for another outburst. Standing in the middle of his cabin, she all but filled the space with her presence, and he awaited her response. Would she acquiesce, or would he throw her to the sharks? Growing impatient, he sighed. "My bath cools, *Mon Chou*. So what is it to be—the sponge or the plank?"

For a few minutes, she remained mute and stock-still. At last, she whirled about, squared her shoulders, and lifted her chin. "The plank."

#

Perched at an impasse, tension invested her frame, as Madalene challenged the captain and tried to ignore his nudity, but never had she glimpsed a naked man, and curiosity beckoned.

Praying for deliverance, for some small measure of compassion from a rogue who seemed bent on unutterable destruction of her character, she clung to the last vestige of hope for survival. But if he tossed her into the ocean, at least she would die, integrity intact, on her terms—not those of a pirate.

"You prefer the company of sharks to mine?" To her dismay, he stormed in her direction, but she held her ground.

"From my perspective, there is little difference, sir." Yes, she intentionally disobeyed Jean Marc's command, as she had nothing to lose.

When he burst into laughter, she jumped but focused her attention on his gaze. "I can see this crossing will be nothing if not entertaining, but you will remain in my cabin, as my guest, and in that I will abide no objection."

"Why?" The prospect terrified her, as she conjured all sorts of horrible fates. "What have I done to you, in our brief acquaintance, to merit such ill treatment?"

"You have to ask?" She did not understand his query. As if they were old friends, sharing countless personal secrets, he retraced his steps, baring a stunning backside that left her clutching her throat, and eased into the tub, and she almost swooned. Then he picked up the bar of soap. "Now you will scrub my back."

"No." She shook her head. "I will not."

"You gave me your word, as a lady, that you would serve me in exchange for passage to Port Royal." Canting his head, he narrowed his stare. "How did you put it? Ah, yes, I remember. You said you coveted compromise and would do your best to perform to my satisfaction, in whatever I commanded of you." He snorted. "So your word means nothing to you?"

"It means everything, as I am a Davies." And he was correct in his assertion, as she said that. But never had she anticipated he would ask so much. "I should have qualified the conditions of our arrangement, as I negotiated in good faith and believed the same of you. And I still do not understand why I must share an accommodation."

"First, this is not a hotel. It is a ship, in the middle of the ocean, filled with randy sea dogs who would love to give you a quick poke." She was not sure what that meant, but she suspected it did not bode well for her. Jean Marc collected a washcloth and again motioned for her to take the item. "Second, as long as you are a guest aboard the Morass, it would be better for you to avail yourself of my protection. If you sleep in this room, the crew will presume you are mine, and they will not touch you." He shrugged. "Otherwise, you are fair game, *Mon Chou.*"

At his pronouncement, she gulped. "Fair game?"

"No prey, no pay, Maddie. And we accept all forms of compensation, especially those of the flesh." With a flick of his wrist, he beckoned, and despite her reservations she took a single step in his direction. "If you wish to partake of my guardianship and, thereby, my cabin and my generous nature, you must obey my orders, as agreed. What is your answer?"

With nary a protest, she stomped to the tub, snatched the soap and cloth, worked up a thick lather, and scrubbed his skin.

"Lower." He chuckled, and she bit back a curse but, oh, what she thought, as she inched further below the water line. "Lower."

Worrying her lip, she stretched long, grazed the cleft of his bottom, and shrieked. Recoiling, she met his taunting expression, flung the wet rag at his face, and fled the quarters.

CHAPTER THREE

A sennight later, anchored just off the coast of a tiny island, Jean Marc handed Maddie to Tyne, who stood in the jolly boat. "Careful, as she is valuable cargo."

"Where are you taking me?" The lady yelped, as she descended the Jacob's ladder and a wave crashed against the hull of the *Morass*, and the smaller craft shifted. With jerky movements, she glanced left and then right. "Are you sure this is safe?"

"Easy, *Mon Chou*. You will be all right." In a flash, he slid down the rope. When he sat on the bench beside her, she scooted so close she might as well have occupied his lap, which was fine with him. "Shove off, Tyne."

"Aye, Cap'n." With another scowl of disapproval, the first mate grabbed the oars and heaved hard.

As they neared the coast, he admired the palms gently swaying in the soft breeze, while she fidgeted and peered over the edge. Ah, his plan worked perfectly, and with a little luck she would sleep in his bed that night. A sharp lurch signaled they landed on the beachhead, and she jumped.

"Oh, dear, are we sinking?" With a death grip on his elbow, she met his stare and widened her eyes.

"No." Laughing, he shook his head, stood, and leaped into the tide. Given her dramatic performance, already the outing was worth the delay. Then he turned, outstretched his arms, and flicked his fingers. "Come."

Just as he expected, she hesitated. "But I cannot swim."

"It is shallow enough that you can walk, *Mon Chou*." At the end of his tether, he cursed, and she gasped.

Wrinkling her nose, she looked on the ocean as though it were some sort of mud pit. "But I will get my dress wet."

To wit he snapped his fingers. "I am waiting."

"You will not be satisfied until you kill me." Grumbling incoherently, she did as he bade.

"Cease the hysterics, as I have no patience for such nonsense." A sack filled with provisions rested at the bow, and he snatched the bag. "Tyne, return for us just after sunset."

"*Return*—wait, where is Mr. Tyne going?" Maddie craned her neck, as he caught her about the waist and led her to the shore. "Jean Marc, what is happening? Am I to be marooned? Are you leaving me to starve?" She wrenched his shirtsleeve. "I will wash your back, I promise."

"How your imagination twists and turns, Madalene." When she dug in her heels, he tightened his hold on her wrist and trudged alee through the dense tropical foliage. "If I were going to abandon you, do you think I would be here, now?"

"I have made no secret of the fact that you frighten me." She shrugged. "And I do not understand how that surprises you, given what you asked of me, this morning."

"You object to something as innocent as brushing my hair?" In that instant, he drew to a halt and prepared to play the ignorant, because he knew precisely what ruffled her pretty little feathers. "Explain how that was offensive."

"You made me stand between your legs, which defied logic, given I could scarcely reach the back length." As he cleared the way with his cutlass, she ducked to avoid low branches. "Are you never reasonable?"

"I am always reasonable." Not to mention savvy, as the position Jean Marc required of her, as she combed his long locks, afforded a spectacular view of her breasts when she bent at the waist. "The real question is why you buck my authority, at every turn, when I have been nothing but a gentleman."

She snorted. "Do you even know what that word—" Her shrill scream pierced the relative quiet. "*A snake.*"

To his delight, she flung herself at him, pressing her feminine curves to his frame, and he savored her lush body. In seconds, he located the source of her distress and chuckled. "*Mon Chou*, that is a harmless creature, and I wager it will not bite if you do not pester it."

"Are you sure, as it appears quite dangerous." Twining her arms about his neck, she buried her face in his chest. "And I would not know, as never have I seen a snake, in my life."

"Then you should rely on my expertise, as I am familiar with these parts." Ever so slowly, he skimmed his palm along her hip, continued to the swell of her derriere, and discovered her fear tempered her awareness. Instead, she shuddered and squeezed tighter. "Please, take me to the ship. I pledge to will do whatever you ask, and I will protest not."

"Why do I doubt you?" Hefting her to his side, he trudged the last few strides and parted the greenery. "Now relax and enjoy the day I have arranged for us."

"I beg your pardon?" As he set her down, she peered over his shoulder and blinked. "Oh, Jean Marc, what is this place?"

"It is an isolated cove, and we must descend carefully, using the rocks as nature's staircase, to the beach crevasse below." Inch by inch, and holding her hand, he preceded her along the rudimentary path. "Worry not, *Mon Chou*, because I will catch you if you fall."

"The water is like crystal and smooth as fresh-pressed sheets." She paused and surveyed the area. "Is the cove completely enclosed?"

"The limestone breaks just beneath the surface, and we should deposit our belongings here, as the tide will rise as the afternoon passes." Using a large boulder as a seat, he stopped and doffed his boots and shirt. As he unhooked his breeches, Maddie averted her gaze.

"What are you doing?" Wringing her hands, she shuffled her feet. "Although I have no knowledge of your motives, and make no claims to apprehend your rationale, just this once, can you remain descent?"

"No." How fetching she appeared, in her pretty pink frock, with her hair piled in charming curls atop her head, and he savored her eventual defilement. Naked, he approached his soon-to-be fallen angel from behind and whispered, "Now take off your clothes, as I intend to teach you to swim."

From the rear, silence reigned supreme when he bargained on additional protest, after he trod into the cool seawater. Checking on his lady, he found her standing stock-still, just as he left her, and her face deathly pale.

"Jean Marc, please, do not make me do it. I am terrified of drowning." A tear streamed her cheek, and he muttered an invective and returned to her. "What I said earlier I meant. Whatever you command of me, I will perform the task, if you let me stay here, where it is dry."

With hands on her shoulders, he rotated her. In seconds, he untied and loosened her laces, as she wept and shivered. "Will you remove the rest or shall I, because you will do as I say?"

A few minutes ticked past, and he tugged on the dress, but she broke free.

"If I cooperate, may I retain my chemise?" she inquired in a small voice.

"It may weigh you down." When she did not budge, he huffed in frustration. "All right, but nothing else."

As he waded into the gentle surf, she used a large outcrop as a makeshift shelter, and he waited. At last, she skittered to the spot where he stacked their things, dropped her bundled garb, and lingered on the beach. Looming in naught but her thin slip, she hugged herself, and he waved for her to join him.

Halfway to him, she paused and cradled her face in her hands, and he realized she harbored genuine fear. So he retraced his path, scooped her up, as he would a child, and carried her into the drink. In a panic, she cried aloud, wrapped her legs about his hips and her arms about his shoulders, and he cupped her bottom through the sheer linen.

"Shh, Maddie. I will not drop you, so you are safe." While fear could be quite provoking, he found nothing arousing in

Madalene's raw terror. Rather, her distress struck a nerve, and he nuzzled her ear as she sobbed. The water ebbed and flowed, and he bobbed with her secure in his grasp. "The shallow ledge drops off, here, so I will maintain my grip. Is this not cool and refreshing, *Mon Chou*?"

"No, it is horrible." Despite his efforts, he could not pry her loose, so he reclined and floated.

"Stretch your legs and kick your feet. Come on, Maddie." Kissing the crest of her ear, he patted her bottom. "Relax, and glide with the tide."

"Why are you making me do this?" With a sniff, she lifted her head, and what he spied in her blue eyes fractured something inside him. "Why do wish to hurt me?"

"You are mistaken, because I am trying to help you." Guilt flared, and she invoked a part of him he had not used in years—his conscience, so he resolved to reason with the stubborn woman. "What if we are attacked, as was the *Trident*, and I cannot defend you? What if I cannot get to you, and you fall into the ocean?"

"I will die." Her sorrowful expression called to him, to some strange yearning he could neither identify nor resist.

"No, you will not." Tipping her chin, he claimed a kiss while she wallowed in a vulnerable state, and he savored the subtle hitch of her breath. "We are going to work together, and by the time we depart the isle, you will swim like a fish, *Mon Chou.*"

As he floated on his back, he tangled his legs with hers and schooled her in the proper technique. Of course, their respective positions coupled with her feminine form and loaded the cannon in his crotch, but she appeared not to notice. Gritting his teeth, and leashing his sordid hunger, he made several laps about the cove.

"You are doing well, Maddie." Whereas he preferred to keep her close, he needed to release her to continue the impromptu lessons. With great reluctance and a wicked erection, Jean Marc separated from her, and she immediately flapped and submerged. In an instant, he yanked her above the surface. "Take it slow, and remember what I taught you."

"I will have your solemn vow not to leave me." In her fear, she almost swamped them, and they both came up sputtering. "I cannot do this."

"Wait." A new idea occurred to him. "Let us return to the shallows." With the sand beneath his feet, and the water lapping at his waist, he stretched out his arms. "Lie down."

"Jean Marc, you are determined to torment me." As she stood upright, he almost dropped to his knees. Wet, her chemise all but disappeared, and he glimpsed a vision that could bring a grown man to tears for want of her. When she obeyed his directive, he offered support but could not stop staring at the cleft in her round bottom. "What now?"

Ah, what he wanted to do to her sweet arse. "Hmm?"

"You are distracted, which does not inspire confidence." She wiggled in his grasp, and he shifted a hand to graze her breast, which elicited another shriek. "Check your behavior, sir."

"My apologies, Maddie." There was the haughty tone he adored. "Now, kick with your feet, and sweep with your arms, in long strokes, and I will support you."

"Like this?" Inexplicably charming in her attempts, she furrowed her brow as she followed his instruction, and he extended praise and encouragement. Little by little, she found her rhythm.

Soon, Jean Marc retreated, and Madalene drifted on her own. Arresting in her excitement, as she made numerous laps, she never hesitated when he prompted her to hold her breath and venture underwater. And that yielded more glorious sights than the sea life, because the chemise shifted and swayed, providing all manner of enticing views of her luscious landscape, and he recalled his true purpose for the outing.

As the sun sat low on the horizon, he collected palm leaves and branches, to start a fire. From the sack, he pulled a blanket, which he spread, and a few other necessities. "Are you hungry, *Mon Chou*?"

"Indeed, given you have exercised me for most of the day." Poor thing had no idea how he intended to employ her, in truth. Rubbing her shapely legs, she frowned. "The saltwater is so harsh, and my skin may never recover."

"Well, I need you to work a bit more, so we can eat." With her hand in his, he walked her to the beach and just into the water. "Have you ever dug for clams?"

"No." She sported a look of confusion. "Yet I gather you will show me, but who will prepare them?"

"Do you think me incapable, Maddie?" Ah, he treasured her countenance of shock, given he had her exactly where he wanted her. "As I have been told I am an excellent cook."

#

So the former pirate fancied himself a chef? How absurd. While Madalene hid behind the rocks to strip off her wet chemise and don her dress, garters, hose, and slippers, Jean Marc pulled on his breeches, a gesture she appreciated, and retrieved various items from his bag. For a few minutes, she studied the fascinating captain.

An odd mix of unpolished charm, equally flawed handsomeness, and an overwhelming aura of larger than life prowess, the bawdy buccaneer could have been a character in Homer's *Iliad*, as one of Achilles' fabled, formidable Myrmidons. In any other circumstance, and with a little refinement, he would have garnered her special attention. Perhaps that was why he frightened her, even as he cooked for her.

After filling a pot with the clams they collected, he uncorked a bottle and poured some liquid over their fare. Then he placed the covered container on the fire and glanced straight at her. "You are watching me, *Mon Chou.*"

"Given the brief tenure of our acquaintance, why do you call me by a term of endearment?" To dry her hair, she removed the pins. Yes, it was shocking to let down her coif before a man who was not her husband, but she had no real choice.

"Because it suits you." In light of his actions, noble in their own way, she wondered whether or not she had been to quick to judge the captain, as he patted the spot beside him. "Come and sit with me."

"In the event I forget my manners later, I will thank you now for the wonderful day." Scooting close, she scrutinized his profile. "How did you injure your eye?"

"In a sword fight." He lifted the lid and stirred the clams. "We are almost ready."

"Why do you wear the patch?" For some reason she could not quite fathom, she ached to comfort him, even though the wound was old, and she reached for him. "May I?"

"You want to see it?" When she nodded, he snickered. "All right."

With the swipe of his hand, he whisked off the leather patch, revealing the full length of the scar, which cut a jagged path from his forehead, through his left eye, which was milky white and ghostly in appearance, and arced across his cheek.

"I like you better without the patch, as it strikes me as rather banal for a former pirate." Trailing her finger along his marred flesh, she smiled. "And you seem far more menacing with it."

"Perhaps I need to appear menacing, to keep the crew in line." From a different bottle, he poured two mugs of rum. "Take a drink with me, Maddie."

"Of course." As opposed to the first time she consumed the none-too-elegant intoxicant, she sipped with care and managed not to choke. "What did you put in the clams to steam them?"

"Ale." After another check of the clams, he set aside the lid and transferred the fare to a large wooden bowl. "Close your eyes."

"What for?" She blinked, as misgivings mounted.

"Do you suppose you can ever do as I ask without questioning my motives?" His scowl chastened her, given his gallantry of late. "Close your eyes."

Despite lingering reservations, she abided his request, and he fed her a morsel. The texture was smooth and chewy, and the taste was a tad salty mixed with other flavors she could not identify, but it was delicious, and she hummed her appreciation. "Jean Marc, that is truly delectable."

"Eat your fill, as you fished them, and there is plenty." How amiable was her host, when away from his ship, and she relaxed. "Would you like some more grog?"

"Yes, please." Indeed, she favored the rum, as the more she consumed, the more she enjoyed it. And it emboldened her. "From where do you hail, and what of your parents?"

"I am from a small town in western France, on the *Seuil du Poitou*, called Poitiers." He gazed into his mug and sighed, and she regretted posing the query. Just as she was about to rescind her question, he lifted his chin. "My mother loved to sit along the banks of Clain River and read to me. I was seven when she died of a fever, and my sire sold me to pay a debt. It was more than a decade before I met him again."

"I beg your pardon?" Her stomach rebelled in that moment, and she drained her mug. "Did you say your father sold you to pay a debt?"

"I did." He uncorked the bottle and refilled their mugs. "The man who owned me was a merchant with a fleet of ships, and he sent me to work loading cargo. It took me eleven years to work off my father's account."

"Oh, Jean Marc, I am so sorry." She could not begin to imagine the horrors he endured, and her heart bled for him. Now she understood the rough exterior and crude language, as that was all he knew, and she vowed to show him kindness.

"Why do you apologize? You did nothing to me." He shrugged, yet she suspected he harbored invisible wounds. "The man was an unholy bastard who loved to whip me for no reason, and his was the first life I ever took, but I did so in self-defense, after he tried to beat me to death."

"But that does not mean I cannot extend a measure of sympathy, and I believe your cause just." Considering what he survived, she viewed him in a completely different light, and she could only imagine the tales he could tell. "In truth, I admire you, as you suffered such adversity at a young age, yet you improved your circumstances, and now you captain your own ship. You must be very proud of your accomplishments."

"What good is pride?" The fire cast shadows on his face, and she noted the angular lines and chiseled cheekbones. "I am still here, and that is all that matters. And I have memories."

"Would you share one?" She inched closer, as she needed to be near him, but she knew not why, and he draped an arm about her waist.

"At night, after *ma mère* tucked me into bed, she used to sing to me." Narrowing his stare, he compressed his lips. "It went something like, *Plaisir d'amour endure qu'un moment, chagrin d'amour dure toute la vie.*" As he continued in his rich baritone that would make many a lady swoon, she joined him for the next verse, and their voices coalesced into a single mellifluous harmony, as together they sang, *"Tant que cette eau coulera doucement vers ce ruisseau qui borde la prairie."* Surprise evident in his countenance, he grinned, and her heart skipped a beat. "You know '*Plaisir d'amour*,' Maddie?"

"Indeed, I know 'The Pleasure of Love' quite well, as it was Aunt Eileen's most cherished composition." Stunned to discover a connection to her errant buccaneer, she revised her opinion of him, as anyone who could recite one of her spinster relation's melodies could not be all bad. "You are a strange creature, Jean Marc, and I no longer believe you are as intimidating as I previously thought." Fondling the soft and supple leather thong, she humphed. "Contrary to your brutish exterior, you gave of yourself to teach me to swim, thereby undermining your repeated threats to throw me into the ocean, you cooked a savory meal as would a beau for his sweetheart, and you crooned in a timbre as smooth as well-churned butter. Indeed, I would argue you wear this patch as a shield, of sorts, not that I blame you, but you are not what you seem, when you drop your guard, and I prefer this side of you, if you permit me to extend the compliment."

"*Mon chou*, that is a pretty sentiment, but I should caution you that your newfound ability will not save you from the sharks." Leaning over her, his nose mere inches from hers, he laughed, and a chill coursed her spine. "So I would not test your supposition, if I were you."

"Of course." Faltering, she slumped her shoulders, gulped, and sought to change the topic. "Have you ever been to Boston?" she inquired in a high-pitched shrill.

"No." Still he loomed, and she pondered how he might respond were she to kiss him. Not that she wanted to kiss him. But she contemplated his reaction were she to enact such a gross breach in polite decorum. At last, he sat upright, and she breathed a sigh of relief. "Why do you ask?"

"Because I think you would love the city." Settling her skirts, she regained a position of relative comfort. "There is a lovely little café on the wharf, and they serve the best sea scallops. We could patronize the teahouse on Blackstone Street, which is the center of the Haymarket, where we could shop. And we could take long strolls along Newbury Street."

"We could?" His lazy smiled mocked her, and it was too late when she realized she had spoken of him as a suitor.

"I apologize for the unintended inference, sir, as I meant no offense." When he pinched her bottom through her dress, she slapped his hand. "Stop that, Jean Marc. I am not your lady, and you are not my—"

"Husband?" Now he guffawed, and she fought tears, but why she knew not.

"That is quite enough." In a huff of indignation, she scrambled to her feet, dusted the sand from her skirts, and sniffed. "Is it not past due for us to return to the *Morass*?"

"Ah, I have ruffled your feathers, *Mon Chou*." Despite his observation, he exhibited no sign of remorse, as he restored his patch. "Alas, I do not court, but if I did, I would pursue you, Maddie." After emptying and rinsing the pot, he rolled the blanket, returned everything to the sack, and smothered the fire. "Now let us walk back to the windward side, where Tyne awaits."

"*Walk*?" With naught but the silver glow of moonlight to guide her, Madalene panicked. "What of the snakes? How can we avoid them if we cannot see them?"

"*Merde*." Grumbling to himself about

frivolous females, Jean Marc grabbed her wrist and pulled her toward a large rock. "Step up, Maddie."

"What for?" When she tarried, he lifted her atop the boulder and then gave her his back.

"I will carry you, now weigh your anchor." He bent at the hips. "Wrap your arms about my shoulders."

"You cannot be serious." In the dark, she rolled her eyes.

"You prefer the snakes?" he stated, haphazardly.

"Hold still." Never in her life had she imagined committing such an egregious infraction of etiquette, but her finishing governess never said anything about pirate attacks, sinking ships, randy buccaneers, and reptiles, so Maddie improvised to survive the situation. When he shifted, she squealed as she hopped aboard her contrived mount. "Oh, how did this happen to me? My mother and Aunt Eileen are probably tossing in their graves."

"Quit complaining, or you may fend for yourself." After retrieving the sack, he braced her legs behind her knees and trudged forth, into the thick jungle foliage.

At some point during the trek, she noted

an altogether foreign but beguiling sensation that built slowly, at first, but quickly erupted into an equally alluring but unfamiliar yearning. Given their respective positions, he rubbed her, albeit unwittingly, in ways no man had ever touched her, and a rush of derring-do bolstered fledgling confidence.

With each advancing stride Jean Marc took, he bounced her, and on the next jolt, she grazed her lips to his ear. A firebrand of heat scorched her veins, and she clenched her thighs about his waist. Beneath her, he flexed his muscles, and she thought she detected a sharp intake of breath.

Was it possible she affected the fascinating former pirate as he affected her?

To test her conjecture, she replicated her strategy in a series of delicate sneak attacks, marveling at each successive response, and she tightened her hold. Resting her chin to his shoulder, she dropped countless accidental kisses on her captain, until he ground to a halt.

"*Mon Chou*, if you wish to seduce me, you should wait until we gain the privacy of my cabin." He chuckled low in his throat, and she felt it all the way to her toes. "Otherwise, if you do that again, you will lift your ankles for me, here and now."

CHAPTER FOUR

As a newborn babe, Maddie slept in Jean Marc's arms as he carried her into his cabin. With his head, he motioned for Tyne to shut the door, because Jean Marc required privacy to enact his plan.

Molten heat simmered in his loins, flared, fanned, and spread through his veins, and anticipation ignited his senses, as he imagined her cries of lust when he took her. Victory, at last, would be his to claim.

In the corner, the hammock remained unused, because never had she been able to reach it, given the height and taut rope. So she slept on the floor, which surprised him, in light of her pampered upbringing and penchant for the finer things in life. But tonight, she would rest between his sheets.

To avoid a scene and her characteristic panic, he eased her to the mattress. In seconds, he divested her of her satin slippers and lace garters, which conveyed an odd mix of allure and delicacy, and he paused to admire the tiny blue bows at perfect center, when he glimpsed her hose.

A flash of tempting visions assailed him, as he recalled the ruche-tipped peaks of her breasts and the dark triangle at the apex of her thighs visible beneath her wet chemise when she swam. Hers had been an achingly sweet attempt at modesty, and he compressed his lips as she turned on her side and smiled in slumber.

Did she dream of him?

Although his fingers itched to strip her bare, and he burned for her, he drew the sheet over her, tucked the cover under her chin, retreated, and wondered what in bloody hell happened to him. Had he lost his mind over a woman?

For a few minutes, he gazed on her, intending to pleasure himself and gain a measure of relief from the torment investing his frame, but he could not inspire himself, though not from lack of want. Indeed, he should rouse her, and make her do it for him, but he could not bring himself to disturb her. How he desired the incomparable Lady Madalene, but he could not take her in her exhausted state. He wanted her awake and alert when he plunged into her softness, that he might relish her screams. At least, that was what he told himself, as he turned and exited his quarters.

Cutting through the maze of lower decks, his soul a mire of conflicting emotions, he wound his way to the waist and ascended to the helm, where Tyne glanced at Jean Marc and glowered.

"How is the gentle lady?" the first mate inquired.

"After the day's activity, she is worn and weary and even now enjoys my hospitality." Jean Marc leaned against the larboard rail and peered at his private sanctuary, the little isle that housed his secrets and offered refuge in times of angst and turmoil. Never had he taken a woman to his safe haven, and he still did not understand why he shared it with Maddie. "Have the crew prepare to ready about."

"Aye, Cap'n." Tyne relayed the orders, and the men scrambled across the boards and into the rigging.

In the past, sailing served to soothe Jean Marc's restless soul, in much the same fashion as marauding fed his baser appetites, when his personal history inflicted the usual inescapable torment. But he wrestled with a new, unfamiliar, and unwelcomed wretchedness, and his preferred balm dozed in blissful oblivion to the danger that lurked in her midst. And he was a danger to her, but perhaps he miscalculated.

Could Madalene pose a greater threat?

"What is wrong?" Tyne propped beside Jean Marc and stared at the moon. "I figured you would be celebrating another successful conquest."

In his mind, Jean Marc replayed their special day. He recalled Maddie's shriek of horror when she spied the snake, and he chuckled. He remembered her appealing blush, as she stood before him in her chemise. And he savored the image of her, which he would carry to his grave, as he gazed upon her succulent body, albeit through the wet linen, for the first time.

"I could not do it," he stated, with an unmistakable air of finality. "But do not ask why, because I cannot explain my actions, or lack thereof."

"I am glad." Tyne scratched his jaw. "Otherwise, you may have incited a mutiny had you brought her back to the ship, in tears. The men watch you, Cap'n, because the lady is nice to them. Indeed, she seems a very fine woman."

"Perhaps that is what concerns me." Nagging anxiety had him rubbing the back of his neck. "Maddie said some things today that I cannot get out of my head." Beneath the indigo blanket of stars, Jean Marc opened the door to his memory and let her dream envelope him. Was it possible? Could Lady Elaine have been correct, when she boldly proclaimed that everyone deserved love? Could he win Maddie's heart, and if he did, what would he do with such devotion? "Have you ever sought an ordinary life on the right side of the law, where you spend your days toiling in a routine not quite of your making? You marry a saucy wench who keeps the marriage bed entertaining, fills your home with squalling babes, and spends your money." He clenched his fists. "But you have something. You have made something that is your own, and no one can take it from you. And never again will you be alone."

"You are not that little boy, anymore, Jean Marc. What your father did cannot be undone, and no one approved of his deed, especially where you were concerned, but the question is how much longer will you allow the actions of another to dictate your future?" Tyne rested a palm to Jean Marc's shoulder. "Let go your anger and give yourself a chance at happiness. If your motives are honorable, and Lady Madalene is obliging, then seize her and do not look back, my friend, as she is a rare jewel. But if you are bent on destruction, then I urge you to find other sport, as you may wreck yourself, along with her."

"What if I am considering a different alternative?" He could not believe what he pondered in that moment, but Madalene gave him hope for a fate he had never coveted, because he never thought it feasible, yet lingering reservations nagged him. And then there was the associative fear. If Maddie believed in him, then he had to prove himself worthy of her faith, and he had to succeed. "Why did you marry Adele?"

"That is a curious question and one I never anticipated from you, but I suppose a woman can alter a man's thinking like nothing else." Tyne chuckled. "The short answer is because I loved her. And had either Adele or our son survived childbirth, I probably would be sitting in the rocker on the front porch of our home in New Orleans, right now, and not a day passes that I do not remember them."

"So you would have been content with a staid existence born of routine?" Jean Marc snickered. "Why do I not believe you?"

"Ah, but there you are mistaken, as there is nothing staid or routine about love and marriage." Shaking his head, Tyne snorted. "Only someone ignorant of the two would make such a ridiculous claim, but I wager you guessed that, if you contemplate a union with Lady Madalene."

"I contemplate nothing." He lied, and he would wager Tyne knew it. Jean Marc raked his fingers through his hair, checked their progress, and stomped to the companion ladder. "Ease fore t'gallant brace six inches, and trim for speed. I am going to bed."

"Aye, Cap'n." Tyne slapped his thigh and guffawed, and Jean Marc all but ran to his cabin.

As soon as he shut the door, the familiar hunger resurfaced, slow and steady, flaring and igniting, until he found himself where he stood, earlier. At bedside, he sat on the edge of the mattress and studied Maddie's patrician profile, so elegant in repose. He swept aside a lock of hair and traced the curve of her cheek, and she mumbled incoherently.

Everything inside him raged, and he ached to claim her. To push her onto her back, rouse her, spread her thighs, and plunge into her pliant flesh before she could protest. To ride her, hard and fast, until she dug her fingernails into his shoulders and screamed with completion. To grab hold of her perfect coif and drive his cock into her mouth. To part the twin globes of her round derriere and seize her bottom. He yearned to possess her, completely, ultimately, every aspect of her.

Instead, he collected a pillow and jumped into the hammock.

#

A sliver of sunlight cut through the portal, and Maddie sighed as she huddled beneath the covers of the comfortable bunk. Then she opened her eyes, glanced from side to side, and shot upright. What was she doing in the bawdy buccaneer's bunk?

"Good morning, *Mon Chou*." Wearing naught but breeches, Jean Marc stood at the washstand and dried his face. "I trust you slept well?"

"You blackguard." After tossing back the sheet, she discovered she missed some items of importance, and the scarce remnants of the future she envisioned crumbled about her. "What happened to my garters and hose?"

"I removed them, to make you comfortable." Without a care in the world, as if he had not ruined her, he strolled to his locker, retrieved a white shirt, and shrugged into the garment. "You were so tired that I did not wish to disturb your slumber."

"And you had your wicked way with me." How could she have been so stupid to invest the smallest measure of faith in the marauder? As she mulled all that she lost in his lustful games, she shuddered. "How could you?"

"How could I—what?" Narrowing his stare, he shifted his weight. "What is wrong?"

"As if you do not know." Emitting a feral cry, she waved her fist in the air. "You taught me to swim, you plied me with food and rum, and you sang to me, all in your illicit quest to destroy my reputation. And to think I trusted you."

"Do you accuse me of something, Lady Madalene?" In that instant, he donned his black patch, which heightened his ominous appearance, and she swallowed hard. "If so, then make your claim, because I behaved honorably."

"Did I or did I not pass the night in your bed?" She summoned high dudgeon. "Forever, you have spoiled my chances for a match, and I shall end my life as did Aunt

Eileen, alone and pining for bygone hopes and aspirations."

"While I hate to disavow you of such sensible conclusions, I did nothing but tend your needs." To her surprise, he seemed genuinely hurt, but he would not fool her again. "And as would a gentleman, which I must confess is new and unfamiliar to me, I spent the wee hours in the hammock."

"I do not believe you." It was then she glanced at the makeshift accommodation comprised of rope and canvas, and she noted telltale evidence—a pillow and crumpled blanket, which all but declared her host spoke the truth. "Oh, Jean Marc, I am so sorry. In a haze of confusion, I leaped to unsupported conclusions woven from whole cloth, and I should make amends."

"What for?" He spat in the basin, and she realized, to her utter amazement, she wounded him. Was it possible he cared for her? "You obviously know me better than I know myself. And while you were quick to note the absence of your undergarments, in your rush to condemn me, you ignored the fact that you still wear your dress."

She glanced down and almost swooned. "You are right. I am still clothed." Choking on contrition, she bit her lip and splayed her arms. "Please, I beg your forgiveness. In my haste, I misjudged you, and I shall go to my grave regretting it, especially after the kindness you extended, yesterday."

"Such is life, *Mon Chou*." With an expression of sadness that wrenched at her heart, he bowed his head, and she would have done anything to rescind her unfounded criticism. "One day you swim in calm, crystal waters, and the next you find yourself battered and beached on the shoals."

"No." Her mind raced, as she searched for means to atone. "You are not battered on the shoals. Rather, my good name lies in the breach, and you must permit me to repair the damage I have inflicted, without cause."

"Why?" His ambivalence cut her to the core. "In three weeks, we will arrive in Port Royal, where you will go your way, and I will go mine. We will never meet again, thus there is no need to concern yourself with pleasantries."

"But it does not have to happen like that." Desperate, Madalene contemplated her options, given her selections were confined to the ship. When she seized upon a brilliant idea, she approached her suddenly reluctant ex-pirate. "Perhaps we could dine here, this evening, instead of with the crew."

"Just the two of us?" His quiet tone, invested with unmistakable pain, slayed her. "Are you sure you trust me enough to eat with you, without a chaperone?"

She deserved that.

"Yes." Never would she have acted so boldly, but in light of her horrible infraction of polite decorum, she had to extend an olive branch. Mustering courage, she took his hand in hers and pressed his palm to her cheek. "If you wish, I will wash your back, and I will personally serve your meal. And if there is another service you require, I shall perform it, to the best of my ability, per our original arrangement."

"And you will smile as you tend my needs?" His skepticism obvious, he arched a brow, and she clenched her gut. "You will neither complain nor refuse my requests, whatever I ask of you?"

Why did she get the strange sensation that he referenced more than food? "On the contrary, I shall count any opportunity to serve you as an honor."

CHAPTER FIVE

There were moments in life upon which he could look back, when he reached the crossroads of fate, and he realized a single choice dictated the course of unforeseeable events for future years. Jean Marc suspected that evening was one of those occasions, because he made a decision where the delectable Lady Madalene was concerned.

As she situated plates and utensils with care, atop the table in his cabin, she hummed *Plaisir d'amour*, evoking fond memories, not that it would do her much good. Vulnerable, when he thought himself immune to such emotions, he simmered in anger given what he viewed as her betrayal. To his amazement, she wounded him when he did not think she possessed the capacity to hurt him, yet he suffered some strange affliction he could not identify, and she would pay in coin of the flesh, after his noble efforts.

On the night he taught her to swim, he could have taken her. He could have been on her and stolen her bride's prize before she knew what happened and voiced a protest, but he altered his tack out of some misplaced sense of chivalry inspired by her pretty words, and he hated himself for it. She weakened him, and he was never weak. Now, she would appease the beast raging inside him, and he would dump her at Port Royal, used and abused, just as he originally planned.

"I am rather new to sea fare, Jean Marc." The evening's entertainment gazed on him and smiled. How charming she was in her contrition, and it would be her eventual downfall. "And you know I have never claimed expertise in the kitchen or the galley, as it were. But Mr. Tyne told me you favor plum-duff, so I had Mr. Allen show me how to prepare supper, just for you. I hope you are hungry."

"In truth, *Mon Chou*, my appetite has waned." Averting his stare, he sighed, as he knew just how to play her, because he wanted her to suffer. "But you should enjoy yourself."

"Oh, but you must eat." In a flurry, she ran to his side and knelt, and he decided he preferred her on her knees. One day soon, she would suck him dry, right there. Leaning on the armrest of his chair, she swept the hair from his forehead. "After your lovely bath, will a hot meal not be the perfect ending to the day?" When he remained silent, she emitted a half-smothered sob. "Please, I beg you. Just a taste, and it will inspire you to dine." She tugged at his wrist. "I filled the bags, myself, and I used extra currants, as Mr. Allen said you prefer the dish double-shotted, as he called it. Does that not entice you?"

Ah, his routine greatly improved in the face of her remorse. That afternoon, when she scrubbed his back with nary a pointed cavil, he also bade her wash his chest, that he might spread his legs and draw her razor-sharp scrutiny to his wicked erection, and his scheme worked beautifully.

An unusual mix of comeliness and intelligence, Maddie presented the ultimate challenge for a rogue of his caliber, and he sincerely anticipated her downfall, as he caught her attention, trapped it, and fed her innate curiosity. In fact, she said nothing when he took himself in hand and fired his cannon. But she watched him. She never took her eyes off him, as his seed burst forth beneath the surface of the water. Instead, she pretended not to notice, but the little pulse beating at the base of her throat declared otherwise.

Indeed, he had her right where he wanted her.

"I shall try, Maddie." He patted her brown curls.

"Wonderful." Her expression brightened, as she leaped to her feet. "I will return with our dinner." At the door, she paused and glanced over her shoulder. "And I should warn you not to overindulge, as I have something very special planned for dessert."

"All right." Jean Marc nodded, as so did he.

The meal passed in relative quiet, as Madalene tried to engage him in conversation, and he resisted her endeavors. As he predicted, she increased her efforts, wheedling and cajoling, at once feeding him healthy morsels, which he met with unimpaired aplomb. But inside he howled with laughter at her gullibility.

Afterward, she stacked the dishes. "Now

you wait here, while I collect our treat."

Adopting the same dreary countenance, he answered with a shrug of his shoulders. Alone, he smiled, as she remained oblivious to his licentious aim, and he licked his lips, as he prepared to feast on her supple flesh. When she returned, he erased all trace of emotion and pushed his chair from the table.

"You are not retiring, are you?" Crestfallen, she set down a covered bowl, and nothing in the world would keep him from enjoying her attempts at recompense. "Because I borrowed on my sewing skills to secure the primary ingredient for our sumptuous dessert, and I do so wish to please you."

Intrigued, though she knew it not, he inclined his head. "What is it?"

"Chocolate mousse." She lifted the lid, revealing an appealing confection. "Did you know Mr. Tyne possesses a horrid sweet tooth and hoards candy?"

"I did." Another notion formed in his brain, one that would benefit his strategy and launch his seduction.

"Shall I feed you?" She dragged her chair closer to his.

"Yes." Ah, it was time for the first strike, and he slapped his thighs. "But you will do so from my lap."

And so he leveled his opening shot.

Maddie stood stock-still, her spine almost as stiff as his cock, and host of emotions flitted through her expression. Then she blinked. "Of course, Jean Marc. As I said, whatever you require."

After scooting the dish to the edge of the table, she stepped about his legs and then settled herself, gasping when he cupped her bottom. Whereas before he had avoided her prying gaze, now he met her stare as she brought a heaping spoon to his lips. When he trailed his tongue across his flesh, she studied his mouth and returned to look him in the eye, and only then did he take what she offered.

And he commenced the dance.

With each successive portion he consumed, her breath quickened, and a sheen of perspiration formed on her brow. To ignite the flames of passion, he alternated bites, taking turns serving her, and a faint blush colored her cheeks, as she shifted her hips and pretended not to notice his rock-hard erection. Tugging at the bodice of her unremarkable yellow frock, she tensed her buttocks, re-deposited the bowl on the table, framed his face, and kissed him.

For the umpteenth time, Maddie shocked him.

It would have been so easy to direct her unschooled movements, but something about the way she touched him, raw but genuine and intoxicating in intensity, held him in check. Tentative with an undercurrent of determination, she was like a baby bird testing its wings before the fledgling flight. With her teeth she grazed his chin, and her glittering blue gaze flared with unmistakable awareness, as she all but demanded his surrender, yet he resisted the urge.

Instead, he reveled in her sweet attack, in her untutored and clumsy caresses, in her moans of unmistakable impatience, as she tried to rouse him, but he clenched his fists at his sides, else the exchange would be over in a matter of minutes, and he preferred to draw out the tender assault.

In inexpressibly adorable desperation, Madalene reached for him with every part of her body, arching her back, pressing herself against him, twining her arms about his neck, spearing her fingers in his hair, and yanking off his leather patch. In opposition to her characteristic elegant mannerisms, she was far from gentle, but he wanted no benevolence from her, and he remained complacent in the face of her aggression, until telltale quivering shook her frame.

Only then did Jean Marc invite her into his mouth with a flick of his tongue, and she responded in kind. It was as if her sails caught wind, as she lurched and bolted, deepening her invasion, licking, suckling, and nipping, signaling her growing ache with a whimper, beckoning with a strangled cry. And that was when he rested a palm to her calf, but she conveyed no notice or dissent.

So he traced tiny circles along the sensitive inner surface of her legs but kept a tight leash on his hunger, as he remained on alert for any sign of demurral. For him, with her, he needed her compliance—needed her acceptance in her eyes when she looked at him, in her arms as she held him, in her expression as he filled her, in her lips as she kissed him, and in her gentle caress as she touched him. He did not know why it mattered, but it did. At her knee, he delayed, he lingered, he took his time with her, and still she displayed no acknowledgement of his salacious advance, so he proceeded.

At last, he grazed the delicate little curls that surrounded the entrance to paradise, and she gasped, but he swallowed it. Now he let go his hunger, let it envelop her, lead her, feed her, and drive her. Given her lack of protest, he brushed and parted her most intimate flesh, and it was then Maddie broke their kiss.

"Do you want me to stop?" Hovering at the point of no return, his voice came to him as if through a dense fog, and he scarcely recognized his tone. On the verge of triumph, he hesitated, and it took everything inside him, every ounce of strength to deny the enticing glory she manifested. Desire sparked, flashed, and spread beneath his skin, as an unquenchable flame, and he longed to brand her as his. But despite his base urges, despite the overwhelming craving, he turned his attention to her and an approval he never imagined pursuing.

Shaking her head, she whispered, "*No.*"

In that instant, Jean Marc plunged into the decadent abyss and took his lady with him. As he grasped the helm and steered them into the storm, he seized her lips. With his tongue teasing and darting, he lured, caressed and inflamed, while he worked magic with his fingers at the apex of her thighs, and she came alive in his lap. Giving himself to the treasured moment, he journeyed beyond the confines of time and space, soaring into a world all their own.

Too soon, Maddie twisted and turned,

stretched long, and went rigid in his arms. Jerking free from his kiss, she met his questioning gaze with a wide-eyed stare, and in her blue depths he spied the wonderment of virgin completion, as she serenaded him with a series of precious yelps and sobs, before collapsing, relaxed, spent, and vulnerable in his embrace.

And that was the time to act, to push her onto her belly, on the mattress, and take her bottom. Awash with insatiable lust and gritting his teeth, he thrust her to her feet, unhooked his breeches, freed his length, grabbed a napkin from the table, and shot his seed into the square of linen.

#

It was late, and Madalene tossed and turned in Jean Marc's bunk, given his insistence that she avail herself of his hospitality, while he occupied the hammock. She knew what kept her awake, what held her in thrall, but she understood it not. In the dark, and beneath the covers, she revisited the strange series of events that led to the heated exchange after dinner and wondered how the buccaneer took command of her body so completely. How he uncovered and connected with something new and exciting she never knew existed within her.

Beneath the sheet, she slid her hand down to the place he wreaked havoc and touched herself, but nothing happened. Passion remained elusive, as fleeting as raindrops after a spring shower. At last, she sat upright.

"Jean Marc, are you awake?" Unseeing, she held her breath.

"Of course. How could anyone sleep with all that noise you make?" He snorted. "What is wrong, *Mon Chou*?"

"What did you do to me, earlier?" Just posing the question gave her a shiver of delight, and she elaborated no more, as she suspected he knew exactly what she referenced.

"I pleasured you." He chuckled. "I set you free, Maddie. Why do you ask?"

"You cannot be serious." She kicked loose from the blanket. "Can you explain it, as I found it fascinating?"

"I gather you have never encountered anything like it." Did he have to use that arrogant tone?

"Did we make love?" Folding her arms in front of her, she pondered the consequences of her behavior. "Am I spoiled?"

"No, we did not make love." Given his response, she sighed in relief. "There are many different ways to achieve completion without the deflowering, and what I did with you is but one. No one need ever know of our games, including a future spouse, unless you tell them."

His reply, simple in its affirmation, sent her reeling, as she wanted to know more of his *many different ways*. "So I retain that which is owed to my fated husband?"

"Indeed, you remain intact." At his rejoinder, she collapsed into her pillow. "And I hope you will not leave something so important to the whim of destiny."

"And can you expound upon what you did to yourself?" That was what she wanted to know most, as his body held her in thrall. "As a particular part of your anatomy does not always appear so...angry. But it perks up when I wash your back, and I know not what to make of what I witnessed this evening, but I must confess you mesmerize me far more than you shock me. Are you surprised, and do you think me a low woman?"

"I could never think ill of you, Maddie." She was so glad he said that. "What you express is a natural, human desire, and there is no shame in your curiosity or your query. Indeed, our bodies were made for pleasure, and what I did for you I did for myself. But there is nothing wrong in sexual fulfillment, and never let anyone tell you otherwise, because often such desire is cursory, while others never taste the heights of ecstasy. It is to be treasured, thus you should celebrate what you experienced."

Oh, she was, in silence.

In her mind, she danced a merry jig, waved her arms in the ear, and sang, *Hallelujah*. But, surely, he did not believe that one intrepid trek into the voluptuous realm would suffice?

"And what if I wish to partake of more?" There it was, her forbidden disclosure spoken in plain terms. She prayed he would not make her provide specifics, as she knew not what she meant. But she needed something to satisfy the burgeoning hunger inciting tumult and turmoil inside her.

Several seconds ticked past, and Madalene, wound tight as a clock spring, feared she might explode. Stretching her legs, she ached in that spot at the apex of her thighs, and she longed to savor his touch, but she lacked the courage to invite him to her bed. But the captivating inclination spiked and speared through her veins, charging every nerve, spreading, fanning the flames of desire.

"There is something we could try, but you must be certain, *Mon Chou*." How could he maintain a calm demeanor, when she wanted to scream? "Perhaps you should consider it, in the light of day, when you are thinking clearly."

"I am thinking clearly." And she was obsessed. Threshing and flailing with newfound passion, she clenched her jaw. "Believe me, I have never been more certain, Jean Marc."

"If I indulge you, I must have your word that you will stop me, if you become frightened or wish to cease the activity for any reason." He had to be joking.

"Know that you have it." She imagined his fingers between her legs, playing her as a finely tuned fiddle.

"Then we will begin your instruction, tomorrow." *Tomorrow*? But she needed him now.

After a few minutes, a soft snore emanated from the hammock, and she expelled a rush of breath in frustration. With her fist, she punched her pillow, rolled onto her side, and she doubted she would sleep a wink.

CHAPTER SIX

"Pull gently, Maddie," Jean Marc whispered in her ear, as she perched between his legs and tensed. "Now, ease up, but not too much. Wait." She paused, as he redirected her movements. "Stroke it, nice and slow. You must tease it, *Mon Chou*. Again. Now, give it a sound yank."

"*Oh*, it is so big." She squealed as she hauled in her first fish, which spattered her dress with water, as it flopped in the jolly boat.

"It is a black sea bass, and it is very good eating." Laughing, he found her delight infectious.

For the past three days, he engaged the society miss in licentious warfare, bringing her to release with his fingers every night, after dinner. Without prompt, she planted herself in his lap and blossomed for him, and as he anticipated, she yearned for more. So that morning, when he woke with his usual stubborn erection, he allowed her to touch him.

At first, she hesitated and just stared at his most profound protuberance. Then she caressed the plum-shaped tip, before grasping him, whole-heartedly. The result had been satisfying if a bit humiliating, because she no sooner put her hands on him than he fired his cannon. Afterward, her thoughts turned to food. Indeed, Maddie was a woman after his heart.

"Shall I catch another one?" She wiggled her bottom, and his loins erupted in flames.

"No." He noted the other boats returning to the *Morass*, and he picked up the oars. "We have enough for dinner."

"And afterward, will you teach me more of lovemaking?" Reclining against his chest as he rowed, she rested her palms to his thighs and squeezed, and he luxuriated in her bold behavior. "Do not forget your promise."

"You believe yourself ready?" Ah, his

scheme worked perfectly, as he needed her to initiate the seduction. "You are prepared to yield your bottom?"

"Are you sure that is normal recreation for a man and a woman?" Angling her head, she cast him a glare of skepticism. "As never have I perceived of such a thing."

Of course, she would not have heard of the licentious act, as he wagered no person of gentle breeding ever engaged in the risqué position, given he had to pay his whores extra to indulge his favored fare, a crude and dirty maneuver he mastered at a young age and relished for its lasciviousness. But when it came to light skirts, Jean Marc preferred the tight bottom hole to the quim, for an elementary reason—as arses produced no bastards.

"Are you so accomplished in the sexual arts?" He snickered at her display of naiveté. "Like I told you, what happens between us is our business, and if you are comfortable with what we do, does it matter what others think?"

"I suppose not." She shrugged, and he relished her ignorance. Then again, he spoke a simple truth, as all he really needed was her consent, and his conscience was clear. "And you would be willing to see it through to its honorable conclusion?"

"Indeed, Maddie." He snorted. As if he would forgo the incomparable sights and sounds of her completion. "No man would leave a lady wanting."

"Have I your word?" Again, she shifted, and he groaned.

"You have it." And he held back any further encouragement, because he had her where he wanted her.

Fidgeting, she dug her fingernails into his muscles, through his breeches. Then she sighed. In his mind, he commenced a silent countdown, as he rowed them to the *Morass*. Just before they reached the hull, she shuffled and peered over her shoulder.

Biting her lip, she tapped his knee in an impatient rhythm. "Must we wait?"

"I beg your pardon?" *Victory.*

"Why do you wish to delay until after dinner?" Wiggling restlessly, she wiped her brow, and he noted the pink tinge of her cheeks and the rapid rise and fall of her bosom. "Can we not begin immediately, as I am uncontrollably excited?"

"If you wish." Despite the lust ravaging his senses and the thrill of anticipation surging in his veins, he mustered an air of ennui. "But you should probably have your bath, first."

"I understand." She averted her gaze. "And then you will come to me?"

It was all he could do to allow her private time to prepare for him. "Yes, *Mon Chou*."

"And you will not make me wait too long?" Her look of desperation almost brought him to his knees, as he lifted her to Tyne while he steadied the Jacob's ladder.

As he gained the waist, he signaled the helmsman, who nodded. To the first mate, Jean Marc said, "Make sail, and you will take my watch, this evening."

"Aye, Cap'n." Tyne sketched a mock salute.

As Maddie made her exit, Jean Marc caught her by the elbow and led her to the bow. "If you are certain you wish to proceed, then I will satisfy you." Struggling with some strange affliction, which defied every attempt to identify or explain, he needed validation from his lady. "But if you have second thoughts, you need only declare as much, and I will not be angry."

"But I have made my decision." Caressing his cheek, she rose on her toes and pressed her mouth to his, unwittingly placing herself in the beast's grasp. "I want to know you, and I am not afraid. All I ask is that you remove that infernal eye patch, as you know I prefer you without it."

"Why do you not like my patch?" He snorted, as no woman ever dared criticize him. "I have been told it makes me appear mysterious."

"I disagree." She whisked a lock hair from his forehead, disarming him with the meager affectation. "You hide behind it, and while that may suffice for others, I will never abide it, as I wish to know every part of you."

In a flash, Jean Marc pulled her into his arms and kissed her hard, as he rocked his hips into hers. An old, familiar hunger flickered and then burst forth, and he rested a palm to the swell of her derriere. He was near, so very near to his triumph, to reclaiming that part of him rendered innocuous by the British and their bloody pact. "Then have your bath, *Mon Chou*, and relax, as it will make what comes later much easier for you. Afterward, I want you to wear nothing but your nightgown, as I would preserve your modesty, for your sake, and your hose with the little blue bows in the back, as I cherish the symbols of your gentle upbringing."

"How do you—no, do not answer that, as I do not believe I want to know." She shook her head and clucked her tongue. "Anything else, my bawdy buccaneer?"

"I want you on your knees, in my bunk, when I arrive." For some odd reason he could not fathom, the overwhelming urge to hold her plagued him, so he refused to relinquish her, just yet. "But you can decline, at any time, and I will stop, *Mon Chou.*"

"I understand." She nuzzled his chest, and he basked in her warmth, which he found both unsettling and comforting. "But as I already made clear, I have no intention of declining, as I want to be close to you."

Her declaration, pedestrian in its construction, spun a web of delicate but nonetheless powerful bonds. She wanted him—all of him, and soon she would have him. Fear reared its ugly head, as he wondered whether or not she would accept what he showed her. Would she desire the man, scarred in more ways than one, or would she reject him? He hoped for the former but prepared for the latter.

In that instant, he released her. "Then go, now."

#

Rinsing the last of the soap from her body, Madalene gazed at the paintings on the wall and frowned. While she never claimed any expertise as an art critic, she considered the crude renderings amateur, at best. Grabbing a towel, she stood. As she dried off, she stuck out her tongue at the naked woman and the couple engaged in some strange activity.

Never would she have considered giving herself to anyone other than her husband, but since Jean Marc agreed to do the honorable by her, which meant it was time to plan a wedding, she had no reservations. No, he was not what she envisioned in a spouse, but she never imagined traveling to Port Royal, surviving a pirate attack, and journeying with her own personal marauder with questionable taste in illustrations.

Then she strolled to the bunk, studied the position, and wondered if the image depicted what Jean Marc intended to do to her. It was then she noted the signature in the bottom right corner, which consisted of the simple initials, JMC.

"Jean Marc Cavalier, pirate painter, swimming teacher, singer, and chef extraordinaire." She giggled as she viewed the depictions in an entirely new light. "What else do you do, my bawdy buccaneer?"

Nervous anticipation drove her to the corner, where she stored the bags with her personal items. After fishing out the hose he requested, she donned the silk and checked the position of the blue bows. She pulled a white cotton nightgown over her head and sat on the mattress to await his arrival.

Biting her lip, she glanced at the pictures, huffed a breath in frustration, and yanked down the offensive representations, as she required no audience, real or otherwise, for the games to come. Twiddling her fingers, she checked her appearance in the mirror he used when he shaved. She collected her brown curls atop her head, assessed her profile, frowned, and freed her locks.

Seconds ticked past, and she paced. When footsteps loomed in the outer passage, she shrieked, ran to the bunk, and adopted the pose he commanded. Behind her, the door opened and closed.

And then there was silence.

"Where are my paintings?" he asked, and she wanted to scream.

"I propped them against the wall, near your locker, as I do not like them." How could he bicker over a couple of scraps of canvas, when she awaited his pleasure?

"You find fault with my work?" His tone hinted at more than a little irritation.

"They are so primitive." She jumped when he rested his hand to the small of her back. "Can you not paint something nice, like fruit or flowers?"

"Fruit or flowers?" He inched the nightgown to her waist, baring her bottom, and the air was cool against her fevered flesh. "Grab a pillow, lie forward, and rest your head, *Mon Chou.*"

That was it, no endearments or romance, just commands.

Following his direction, her new posture left her exposed and vulnerable, and she buried her face in the cushion.

"You hide from me." He placed the briefest kiss on the back of her thighs. "Are you ashamed?"

"No." She shook her head and turned to the side. "I am not sure what I feel."

In that, she spoke the truth, as so many sensations speared beneath her flesh, unfurling, fanning out, searing every part of her, and he had yet to touch her where she wanted his attention most. But it was the promise of something more that emboldened her. She would not retreat.

"And you still want to surrender your arse to me?" How could he be so nonchalant, when she was ready to explode with uncontrollable excitement? To her exasperation, he made no contact with her.

"*Yes.*" Simmering, aching with need to be

possessed, to be his lady, she moaned.

"This is oil, Maddie." Massaging the slippery substance into her skin, he finally caressed her derriere, and she hummed in appreciation. "It will make the first time much easier for you. But before we begin, I must have your pledge that you will stop me if I hurt you or you change your mind. Now, tell me you understand, else I will go no further."

"I understand." Drowning in passion, awash, inundated, she yielded in that moment, though he knew it not.

And so he embarked on their new and enticing endeavor, driving her, inciting her, luring her into his world of unbridled debauchery with a series of salacious strokes and kisses in unmentionable places, and she pined for him, shedding her polished exterior to function as molding clay, that he might make her what he wanted.

With unrestrained abandon, she threw herself into his path, she taunted and teased, summoning the marauder with a wiggle and an overwhelming need to surrender, to be his, to be the one taken. When he parted her bottom and smoothed the oil along her cleft, she tensed, and then there was decadent pressure, foreign yet beguiling. Determined and demanding.

Jean Marc grasped her hips and thrust, and she cried out from the shock, as opposed to pain. As he entered her, slow and steady, he stretched her, filled her, possessed her, and stripped her of any fragment of civilized behavior, and she reveled in the intimate invasion.

In unwavering submission, she spread wide her legs, and he curled about her, his thighs trapping hers, and played an arresting accompaniment with his fingers at her core, stoking the flames of lust. A sensuous symphony comprised of her breathy sighs and his guttural groans formed an intricate tapestry, perfectly melding with the repetitive slap of his flesh to hers. So she held naught back from her man, and in the giving she received steadfast acceptance, encouragement, and incomparable satisfaction, and Madalene soared higher, farther, and faster than she ever thought possible.

To his unerring praise, she discarded her inhibitions, cast off the social expectations that stifled free expression and escaped the invisible yet potent restraints into which she had been born. And so she unleashed her impulses, obeyed her titillating inclinations, and tensed to meet his rhythmic bump and grind.

With her pirate captain, she altered, she changed; she became something altogether different. No elegant façade born of years in study, no polished garments, no polite manners, no mask shielded her carnal cravings. She yielded everything to Jean Marc. For him, she functioned as a sensate being, pliant, adaptable to his yearnings, and resilient, to be cast and recast in the image he desired, and in so doing, Madalene found herself.

CHAPTER SEVEN

A sennight had passed when Jean Marc stirred in his bunk and then stilled, as he did not want to wake Maddie. Dozing in his arms, her favorite resting place, she remained oblivious to his scrutiny, as he studied her face, the classical lines, elegant curves, and cute little nose. What was it about her? Why did she fascinate him?

Because he cared for her.

Somewhere between teaching her to swim, to fish, to tie knots, and to read a map, something happened to him, and he was not sure he appreciated it. Emotional attachments were new and unfamiliar seas, and much like the sharks that lurked just beneath the calm surface of the water, such devotion crept up slowly, in silence, and overtook its prey before the possibility of escape presented itself. Indeed, there was no evasion, no eluding the tenuous but infallible bonds that snared him.

His first instinct was to fight, to struggle, to deny the gossamer prison, impervious to flight, in which he dwelled. Affection asked no permission and sought no admittance. It spawned, took hold, rooted, and lived within him, despite intentions to the contrary.

It was supposed to be an easy conquest. Raid and pillage. He had done it before on occasions too numerous to count. But this particular invasion had been different from the start, as never had he taken a well-bred virgin. In truth, she remained intact, as he had not sailed her honey harbor.

But he claimed her windward passage every morning and night, and sometimes in between. That was his plan, was it not? He schemed to defile an innocent and prove he remained in control of his life, despite the pact with the Crown. It mattered not that he desired her; at least, that was what he told himself.

And Maddie never rejected him. Rather, she delighted in his baser instincts, often provoking him to ravage her, luring him to their cabin with a sultry, come-hither stare or a whispered plea, and he answered her summons. She spurred him, she incited him, but most of all, she accepted him.

Yet, for him, with her, the more he took from her, the more he seized, captured, and consumed, the more he lacked. And while he fought with a seemingly insatiable hunger, his society miss came to him with her characteristic poise and assurance and without complaint. With a glance or a snap of his fingers, she bared her beautiful bottom and welcomed his lascivious invasion. Indeed, nothing about the situation made sense, as she was not supposed to enjoy his depravity, yet she reveled in it.

"A penny for your thoughts." Nuzzling his neck, she giggled and walked her fingers down to caress his erection. "Or should I roll onto my side, my bawdy buccaneer?"

"Not yet, *Mon Chou.*" Something bothered him, as she made endless references he did not quite understand. Although he meant to inquire about her comments after dinner the previous evening, as usual, she distracted him, and they uttered naught incoherent. "Yesterday, when you talked about living in Boston, and redecorating the master suite in your home for us, to what were you referring?"

"Oh, dear." Reclining on her back, she focused on the ceiling and sighed. "I was afraid you might protest, but I want to live in the city where I was raised. All my friends are there, and I know we will be the height of the social season. Is that a problem for you?"

"Why would it be a problem for me?" Indeed, she spoke gibberish, and he shrugged. "You may continue to live wherever you wish, as you are your own person, Maddie."

"So you are amenable?" With a squeal, she hugged him. "Jean Marc, you make me happy, do you know that? And no one is more surprised than I, as you are not what I envisioned when I dreamed of my knight in shining armor, coming to rescue me."

"He did not wear an eye patch and carry a pistol?" She worked him then, stroking, squeezing, provoking, and he relished her desire. "You have grown so bold, *Mon Chou*, and I like it."

"It is your licentious tutelage, my pirate." She squirmed, as he fondled her tiny pearl at the apex of her thighs. "And I love it when you touch me." Angling her head, she pressed her lips to his nipple, and he shuddered. "I suppose it is fortunate that I want a large family, as I suspect you will never tire of begetting babes, but we should wait to conceive until after we are married."

And so Maddie stole the wind from his sails.

At first, he had no idea how to respond, as it dawned on him that he had grossly miscalculated. But with her singular clarification, their conversations suddenly developed a clear and concise discernment, with no room for error.

In a flash, he transported to their fledgling fishing lesson and her simple statement, when she opted to yield her arse: *And you would be willing to see it through to its honorable conclusion?*

Madalene's definition of 'honorable conclusion' varied drastically from his, as he referenced completion, while she referred to a wedding. But Jean Marc was in no position to take a wife. He remained a wanted man, despite the promise of a pardon, until he completed a year of virtuous behavior. Then he wondered why he even considered a union.

"What is it, my darling?" Covering his mouth with hers, she drew him deeper into the blissful paradise she manifested. "Are you afraid my friends will not welcome you?"

Incapable of speech, he nodded.

"Poor Jean Marc, they will adore you, as do

I." Glowing, she moaned as he caressed her breasts through the nightgown she insisted on wearing. "And I will never leave your side, so you have nothing fear. We will partake of all the delights of Boston, and I want to travel to the tiny cove, where you taught me to swim, as I have come to think of it as our special place. We can spend winter at Fair Winds and summers in the city. Does that not sound delightful?"

For the next several minutes, Maddie prattled on about myriad social affairs, venues, and locales she wished to share with him, and he imagined himself as her husband, garbed in gentlemen's attire.

He envisioned himself beside her at the theatre, in the carriage as they rode about the streets, arm and arm as they strolled the Commons, and behind her as she engaged in her litany of charitable events. More importantly, he wanted her, and he ached to give her the dream.

To his surprise, she adopted the requisite pose, and he came alert when she wiggled her derriere in unmistakable invitation. "Please, Jean Marc. Just thinking of our future excites me, and I cannot wait any longer."

It was a daunting realization that he provided the source of so much contentment and elation to one person. To need and be needed, in return. Never had he brought anyone satisfaction that extended beyond the realm of seduction and sexual gratification, and he comprehended, in that moment, Maddie's idea of 'more.' He wanted that for her, but he doubted his ability to fulfill her fantasy, and that hurt him more than he wanted to admit.

Emitting a sob of impatience, she nudged him.

"Very well, *Mon Chou.*" He spat on his hand, wet the tip of his cock, spread her bottom cheeks, positioned himself at her opening, thrust, and gave her all he had to offer.

#

It was late in the afternoon when Madalene rose from a nap, exhausted in the wake of Jean Marc's penchant for long morning rides, and frowned. At the washstand, she poured water into the basin and wet her fevered brow. The cabin seemed to spin out of control, and she soaked a cloth, carried it to the bunk, pulled back the covers, and gasped.

A small crimson stain marred the white sheet, and she twisted and turned, only to discover another mark on her nightgown. Unsure what to make of the curious development, she stripped the mattress and collected clean bedclothes. After refitting the bunk, she piled the soiled cotton at the basin and attempted to scrub out the blemish. But once again she lost her balance, and she sat on the floor to gain her bearings. That was where Jean Marc found her, when he returned to his quarters for lunch.

"Maddie?" To his credit, he ran to her. "What happened, *Mon Chou*? Are you all right?"

"I am not sure." She shifted. "But I am bleeding."

"*Merde*." He assessed her condition, lifted her into his arms, and carried her to the bunk, where he deposited her with care. "Merde. Merde." With remorse investing his countenance, he raked his fingers through his hair. "I hurt you, my delicate flower, and I am so sorry." As he retraced his steps, he said over his shoulder, "Wait there, as I will be back."

Confused by his reaction, but too spent to argue, she drifted on the fringe of sleep when he stomped into the cabin. Bearing two steaming buckets, he trudged to the tub and emptied the water, and she yawned.

"But I am too tired to bathe, Jean Marc." Stretching long, she wiggled her toes and basked in his attention. "I fear I might drown."

"That is no concern, as I will not leave you." That brought her alert, as he grabbed the soap and a cloth from the washstand.

"You wish to remain?" She blinked, as he dragged a chair into position, that he might serve her. "You would wash me?"

"*Mon Chou*, I have taken your bottom too roughly, to the point that I injured you." He snorted. "Do you think it not a little late to be shy with your body?"

"But, it is not done." Before she could protest, he drew her to her feet and whisked the linen garment from her. Covering her breasts, she pulled her legs together, and then she wondered why she fought shyness with him. "Upon my word, but you are the bawdiest buccaneer I have ever known."

"I wager I am the only true buccaneer you have ever known, so that is not saying much." With his hands at her waist, he hefted her into the bath. "Now you will take a long soak, and I will fetch our meal. Then you will retire early, as you must get better, and there will be no night games for us until you heal."

"You cannot mean that." She sank beneath the warm water and sighed, as she ached in places she never realized she could ache. "I shall tempt you, sir, and you will take me."

"Do you presume to give me orders, Maddie? As I recall, I am the captain of the *Black Morass*." No doubt he intended his brooding expression to incite fear, as he planted fists on hips and stared down his nose at her, but she could only giggle. "What am I to do with you?"

"Why, what you always do with me." Yes, she baited her rogue pirate, as she loved his particular brand of ravishment, and it was a hard habit to break. Since he agreed to marry her, she had nothing to fret, on that account. "Is that so wrong, because you claim it is quite natural?"

He opened his mouth and closed it. "I have well and thoroughly corrupted you, *Mon Chou*, and I am not certain that is a good thing."

"You liked it last night and this morning." She could not help but laugh, as he muttered invective in French and stormed out the door.

After a lovely respite, she perched atop a fluffy pillow, in Jean Marc's lap, and he fed her bits of goose and truffle pie, interspersed with tantalizing kisses and tender caresses. And in those quiet moments of cherished overtures, she opened her heart and let it sing.

Indeed, Lady Madalene Davies had fallen in love with a bawdy buccaneer.

The only thing that tempered her happiness was the unknown. Would he permit himself the luxury of loving her, in return? Then again, he withheld nothing from her. Perhaps Jean Marc was not the problem.

Since she decided to break with decorum and yield part of her anatomy to her captain, she held one aspect in reserve. She refused him the bride's prize, owing to a proper ceremony and the requisite vows. Why should he surrender what she wanted, when she denied him that which he coveted most? But how could she initiate the seduction, when she dealt with a past master in the sexual arts?

Therein hid the answer.

"So what shall we do, given you eschew your favorite pastime?" She placed a series of kisses along the scar on his face and removed the patch she detested. "Should I read to you?"

"I have no books." He arched a brow. "We could play cards."

"But I am terrible at such games." And she recalled the shocking images on the deck. Pretending to give the query ample consideration, she tapped a finger to her chin and then snapped her fingers. "I have a lovely idea. You could paint my portrait."

"You would pose for me?" He appeared startled. "You would sit, that I might render your beautiful face on canvas, *Mon Chou*?"

"Indeed, it is the least I can do, given I forbade you from displaying the others." Of course, she planned to model far more than her profile, and she had her marauder right where she wanted him. "Why do you not collect your paints and palette, and I will assume an advantageous stance to inspire you."

"All right." He eased her from his lap. "Are you feeling better?"

"Much, in light of your special attention." As he foraged for his supplies, she doffed her nightgown, pulled the few pins from her messy coif, and reclined on her side in the bunk. It was time to commit to Jean Marc as he committed to her.

After gathering his things, he set the items on the table, took up his palette, turned to her, and dropped the thin board to the floor. "No, *Mon Chou*. Your bottom is injured, and I would not harm you further."

With her knuckles, she grazed her breast, as he never could resist her bold behavior. "But there are other things we might do."

Myriad emotions invested his countenance, evidencing the war raging inside him. "Such as—what?"

"You can accept my maidenhead," she said, in a whisper. "I give it to you, of my own free will, without any reservations. I give you all that I am and more, if only you will embrace me."

For a few minutes, he just stood there and stared at her. "Why?"

"Because I love you." It wounded her that he thought himself undeserving of her gift. "As we are to be married, what does it matter when we consummate our union? And as you stated, quite rightly, what happens between us is our business."

"Trust me, it matters a great deal." He licked his lips and bared his teeth. "We should not do this."

"I disagree, and I want you." Bolstered by newfound resolve, she flicked her fingers in entreaty. "Oh, open your heart to me, Jean Marc. Give me a chance, as I will never disappoint you."

"I believe in you, *Mon Chou*, and I hold dear your dream. But you are not the one I doubt." Yet he fought her, as he lingered. "Are you certain this is what you want?"

Considering his ribald manners, his sudden

reticence surprised her.

"Yes." He approached, and she grabbed his wrist and pulled him down to her. "Tonight, I wish to look upon your face as you make love to me. But in light of all we have shared, thus far, this is naught but a formality, as I long to be yours."

On all fours, he crawled over her and then gave her his weight, and she thrilled to his warmth. Framing her face, as she wrapped her legs and arms about him, he kissed the tip of her nose. "*Mon Chou*, you were mine the moment I found you on the *Trident*."

CHAPTER EIGHT

It was a sunny, clear morning when the *Black Morass*, to its captain's great reluctance, pulled into Port Royal. At the entrance to the bay, a British Navy vessel signaled, and Jean Marc waved at the helmsman. "Heave to and yield."

"Who goes there, and state your business?" inquired a lobster of rank.

"I am but an honest fisherman providing assistance to a citizen of His Majesty." Jean Marc glanced at Tyne. "Go below and fetch Lady Madalene. Be sure to collect her belongings."

"Aye, Cap'n." The first mate dipped his

chin and navigated the companion ladder.

And so began a slow, painful descent into hell, in stark contrast with the heavenly past sennight spent in Maddie's arms, as Jean Marc launched the final act of his plan. Yet, so much had changed, and a lethal mixture of regret and remorse ravaged his gut. At a crossroads, he vowed to be strong for his woman, and she was his woman, but he had to sacrifice his own happiness to ensure hers, even if it killed him, and it might.

"During a trip to the American Carolinas, I happened upon a ship in distress, aboard which a young woman clung to the stern rail." Jean Marc recalled her history. "She claims her father resides in Port Royal. His name is Lord Nigel Davies, earl of Livingston."

"If you will prepare your mainsail hull, you may transfer the lady into our custody, and we will deliver her to Lord Livingston." The soldier barked orders to his men, and Jean Marc did the same.

At the waist, he met Maddie for the last time.

It was in those few minutes that he realized it would not be so easy to let go, as he presumed. Indeed, the nobler choice struck a mortal blow, and he clung to his sanity by mere tenterhooks. But when she appeared, garbed in another of her modest gowns, with a matching bonnet trimmed in lace, his knees buckled, and he gritted his teeth.

"Oh, Jean Marc, I am so excited, and you have made me inexpressibly happy." Bouncing on her toes, she favored him with a shimmering smile, and what he would do to maintain that glow. "And I just know my father will adore you, as do I." Grasping his wrist, she dragged him to the plank. "We must hurry, as I want to begin the next chapter in our life, as a couple." She smoothed her skirts and fidgeted with her gloves. "Do you think we can marry by the end of the week, as I long to be your wife? And would you prefer a wedding on the beach, with your crew in attendance, or something small and private?"

"Maddie, wait." He drew her to a halt, and something inside him fractured in that instant. "I must speak with you."

"Silly man, whatever it is, can you not discuss it with me after we arrive at the plantation, as I am uncontrollably exhilarated at the prospect of introducing you to my father?" When she met his stare, her enthusiasm waned. "For goodness sake, Jean Marc, you look as though you just lost your best friend. What is wrong?"

"I must bid farewell, *Mon Chou.*" The imaginary cracks and fissures grew and spread, tearing at every part of him.

"What? Are you mad?" Furrowing her brow, she retreated a step, and her glorious glimmer dimmed. Then her expression sobered, and he braced for dramatics. Instead, she compressed her lips, stretched tall, adopted her polished and poised veneer he had come to adore, and lifted her chin. "*Oh*—you never intended to marry me."

It was a statement, not a question.

"No." And it slayed him to admit it, but for her sake he had to preserve the deception, because she would never leave him if she knew the reality. If she comprehended the depth of his regard. If she understood what she had come to represent in his life. "Yet you should not grieve for what might have been, as we had fun, you and I."

"Fun?" She swallowed hard, and her chin quivered. "But I love you."

And never had he thought it possible that she would grant him such an honor.

"More's the pity, as I never asked for your heart, Maddie." That was supposed to have been his victorious triumph, the moment of her ultimate downfall, and yet the reverse was true. She would cry, stomp her feet, pummel him with righteous indignation, and he would reclaim the marauder of old, the barbarian the British gelded would survive to ravish another innocent and prove he still controlled his destiny. Instead, he longed to be something else—he wanted to be her knight, her hero. That he failed her so miserably cut like a knife, and an invisible but nonetheless potent grip clutched his throat and threatened to choke him. "Your dream is just that, a fantasy. Were I a gentlemen, I should never have let you labor under the ridiculous belief, but you know exactly what I am, so there are no illusions."

"All right." Inhaling a shaky breath, she extended her hand, as would a gentleman, despite her crestfallen appearance, and his admiration for her grew by leaps and bounds. "If that is all it was to you, then that is all it was to me." Her proclamation ran through him as the sharpest sword. "Goodbye, Jean Marc. I wish you well."

And so his grand conquest died in the flames and rubble, bested by the quiet strength and unimpeachable honor of a gentle society miss who preferred lace-collared frocks to breeches. The comeuppance, the worst of his life, was nothing less than he deserved, but she did not belong in his world.

She was an exquisite flower amid a vast and barren desert, and he had to relinquish her.

As he stood at the starboard rail, she exchanged bits of conversation with various members of the crew, all of whom doffed their hats, and paused to kiss Tyne on the cheek. With the grace and elegance that pervaded her every gesture, she turned and addressed the men, as a whole.

"Thank you, for saving my life and treating me with such kindness. I owe you a debt I can never repay." Then she pinned Jean Marc with a steely glare. "And I will never forget you."

And then Maddie was gone.

The ensuing hole in his universe, marked by her sudden absence, opened and gaped wide, jeopardizing the foundation upon which he built his stage, portending the ominous intent to swallow him whole. And although he had not wept since the day his father delivered a young Jean Marc to his new owner, his eyes welled with unshed tears.

If only she had played her part, but the mere wisp of a girl outwitted him, and in the process she vanquished her would-be vanquisher. For a while, he remained rooted to the spot, hoping to glimpse her aboard the naval ship. Impatient, he craned his neck and then caught sight of her in a skiff, accompanied by three redcoats, as a deckhand rowed her to the docks.

Each successive rise and fall of the oars increased the space between them, yet he maintained his post, struggling to preserve the connection, however fleeting. And although he could not see clearly, he swore she watched him. A dull ache flickered in his chest, the pain increasing in direct proportion to the ever-growing distance from his dainty Madalene.

Weighted by some mystical burden, which tightened its stranglehold about his throat, squeezing, choking, threatening to wring the air from his lungs, he clutched tight the rail but found no relief or support. Instead, the invisible torment delved deep into his gut, unfurled, and spread, compounding the agony ravaging his soul, and he fought for breath.

When she reached her destination, she disembarked and disappeared in the crowd, and he dug his nails into the wood rail. It was time to admit the real reason he rejected her, and it had nothing to do with pride, plunder, or possession. "I am sorry, *Mon Chou*, but I had to surrender you. I am a wanted man, and I could not endanger you, because I love you, too."

Tyne cleared his throat. "Have you decided on a new course, Cap'n?"

There were countless journeys Jean Marc could have chosen, but he could not respond, as all he wanted was Maddie. The only salve to successfully soothe the barbarian within had left him, at his idiotic urging, but he evoked the chorus of her sweet sighs and sultry moans, as she threw herself into his charge without care for her safety. Indeed, she manifested the perfect contradiction of refined mannerisms and fearless audacity, and she spoke to him on some inscrutable level that defied every definition. Most importantly, she loved him.

Drowning in seemingly eternal damnation on earth, he emitted a feral growl of disgust, snapped to attention, cursed himself a fool, and pushed from the rail. "Take us to the windward side and drop anchor, as we will go ashore just after dusk. And if you wish to retain use of your teeth, you will wipe that smirk off your face."

#

It was early in the afternoon, as British Army Lieutenant Lowe steered the wagon past a stately stone gate, which bore a sign marked, The Fair Winds, and Madalene hugged her sacks of personal belongings and tried to ignore the heartache that threatened to tear her in two.

How could Jean Marc abandon her, after everything they shared. After the past sennight. After she gave him her body. After she surrendered her maidenhead. After she gifted him her heart, he dropped her into the custody of the English and sailed away, as though she were nothing, and she died a little inside, every time she reflected on his rejection.

At the end of a long and sandy drive, lined with palm trees, loomed a large, two-story house with six massive columns spanning the front, a balcony rimmed by wrought iron railing at top center, and black shutters framing each window.

If she had any assumptions regarding how a plantation house should look, the Fair Winds exceeded her expectations. When Lieutenant Lowe reined in, a dark-skinned woman appeared at the door and then disappeared inside the home. Shortly thereafter, an older gentleman and a young lady strolled onto the porch.

"Let me help you, Lady Madalene." Lieutenant Lowe jumped to the ground and then turned to hand her down. "Lord Livingston, I have brought your daughter to you, safe and sound."

"Madalene?" The grey-haired, distinguished elder with familiar blue eyes, which welled with unshed tears, pressed a hand to his chest. "Is that you, dear child?"

"Papa?" She dropped her things and ran into his waiting embrace. "Oh, Papa, it has been so long, and I have prayed for this day."

"My darling girl, at last we are reunited." At first, he hugged her, but then he held her at arm's length. "Let me look at you. You are the very image of your mother, God rest her soul."

"What is *she* doing here?" The pregnant blonde cast a countenance of unmasked loathing and cradled her large belly. "And how long is she staying?"

"Now, now, Prudence." Papa chuckled. "Am I to be caught in the middle of two strong-willed females?" With a twinkle in his stare, he drew Prudence, who appeared not much older than Madalene, to his side. "Allow me to introduce your stepmother, Lady Prudence, countess of Livingston."

"It is a pleasure to make your acquaintance, Lady Prudence. Forgive my surprise, as I did not know my father had taken a new wife." Fighting to conceal her shock at the revelation, Madalene sketched a quick curtsey.

"I look forward to getting to know you, Papa, and what I presume is my future brother or sister."

"Thank you, for bringing my daughter to me." Papa shook Lieutenant Lowe's hand and sent the soldier on his way. "Shall we adjourn to the drawing room for a bit of refreshment?"

After consuming a glass of lemonade heightened with sweet marsala, during which time she shared her woeful tale of the *Trident* and Captain Hammond's demise, to her father's horror, Madalene recounted her rescue and subsequent travel aboard the *Black Morass* but omitted her relationship with Jean Marc. Indeed, she had no relationship with the pirate captain, given his rejection.

"Might I be shown to my chamber, Papa?" Madalene rubbed the back of her neck, as she faltered beneath Lady Prudence's unveiled perturbation. "It has been a terribly lengthy journey, and I am in dire need of a nap."

"Of course, my child." Papa stood and kissed her forehead. "Miss Hannah will take you to your accommodation, and we will talk more over dinner."

"I suppose she wants the best room in the house." Scowling, Prudence scrutinized Madalene from top to toe. "As if she is an honored guest."

"And so she shall have it." To the housekeeper, Papa said, "Install Lady Madalene in the suite at the south end, which overlooks the ocean, and see to her every comfort." Then at his wife, he wagged a finger. "Prudence, do not ever take that tone with my daughter. Madalene is my firstborn, and her position demands respect. You will act as befits your station, or you will suffer the consequences of your ill manners. Do I make myself clear?"

To wit the not so nice stepmother stomped a foot in protest.

As Madalene climbed the stairs, Miss Hannah smiled. "Your grandfather, Mr. Crawford, was a very fine man, if I may say so, Lady Madalene."

"Thank you, Miss Hannah." She admired the wood grain of the polished balustrade. "I miss him still. And Aunt Eileen spoke highly of the Fair Winds. I am sorry I never ventured here, with her. Have you worked here very long?"

"I have proudly served three generations of Crawfords." The housekeeper averted her gaze. "The Fair Winds was the first plantation in Port Royal to hire paid workers, as opposed to purchasing slaves, and my parents are buried in the family cemetery, alongside your uncle, Archer Crawford."

"I wish I had known him, as Aunt Eileen told the wildest stories about Archer and his Saturday morning polo matches." Steeped in history, the grand residence boasted paintings of Madalene's ancestors, and she wished Jean Marc was with her to share the experience.

On the second floor, the landing spread wide, revealing an expansive hallway. At the third door on the left, Miss Hannah propped ajar the oak panel, strolled to the far wall, drew back the drapes, and flung open the sash. A burst of sea air mixed with the scent of kelp enveloped Madalene, harkening cherished memories aboard the *Morass*.

"Shall I unpack your bags, Lady Madalene?" The housekeeper stood with hands clasped before her.

"No, thank you." The soul-shattering sorrow that plagued her since Jean Marc broke her heart loomed on the horizon, and she preferred privacy, in that moment. "I would like to rest. Would you call me in time for dinner?"

"Yes, Lady Madalene." At the entrance, the housekeeper paused. "The staff prayed for your safe arrival, and I will tell them of your presence. I will leave the door open to properly cool the room, and you may close it when you lie down."

"Again, my thanks, Miss Hannah." Madalene sat on the bed and doffed her slippers. "I look forward to improving our acquaintance."

Gazing out the window, Madalene noted a ship in the distance, and she ran to the ledge. Was it the *Black Morass*? Was Jean Marc out there, somewhere, thinking of her? Did he pine for her as she yearned for him?

And how she ached for him, for his arms about her waist, for his lips on her mouth, for his hands on her body. Did he miss her even a little? Given his dismissal, she doubted he spared her a second thought, and that hurt.

A gentle breeze whispered and thrummed, sifting through her hair and kissing the tears that streamed her cheeks. "How could you?"

"How could I—what?" Prudence inquired.

Dragging her sleeve across her face, Madalene whirled about. "Oh, it is you."

"Why did you come here?" Madalene's stepmother paced as a caged animal. "What do you want from us? The Fair Winds is ours, and I will not let you take it from us, as it is my child's legacy."

"I beg your pardon?" Anger sparked, but Madalene checked her temper. "You labor under the misapprehension that this land is part of my father's entailment, Lady Prudence. On the contrary, the Fair Winds is one of the gems in the Crawford estate, which I inherited, by law, from my Aunt Eileen. While I have no plans to evict you from the plantation, I will brook no interference in my affairs and, in future, will thank you not to insert yourself into my business."

"How dare you, grasping, greedy schemer. What right have you to this property, which you have never worked?" Lady Prudence leveled a malevolent stare. "You will not succeed, if you try, as I will stop you. You will not rob my babe of its deserved fortune."

"And what gives you standing in the matter, given you never labored for Fair Winds?" Madalene pointed for emphasis. "Now get out, and I warn you not to impinge on my person, again, else you will regret it."

"Do not worry." The termagant smiled, and Madalene's skin crawled. "I will have no need to bother you."

With that, Lady Prudence slammed shut the door, and Madalene shuddered. Crawling atop the mattress, she hugged a pillow, closed her eyes, and summoned a vision of Jean Marc. Then she unleashed her misery, and grief rushed forth as a tidal wave.

CHAPTER NINE

The sun sank below the yardarm on the third full day without Maddie, and Jean Marc feared he might run amok. After canvassing Port Royal for any mention of his woman, he ventured to the local whorehouse for a drink and a quick fuck with a three-penny upright. At least, that was his plan.

In the crowded brothel, some of the worst of humanity mingled, smoked, and indulged their baser appetites, while a musician screeched and scratched on a violin. The dank stench of sweat mixed with stale ale and the telltale odor of sex, and he second-guessed his tack, until he spied a familiar face in the back corner.

"Barry, what are you doing here?" Jean Marc pulled up a chair, sat, and flagged a bar wench for a glass of rum. "I did not think you traveled these parts, for fear of capture."

"Jean Marc, it is good to see you, old friend." The pirate, known as the Iron Corsair on the seas, scratched his chin and gnawed on a roasted turkey leg. "And you are the last person I expected to walk through that door."

"My fortunes changed, I have a new mission of unparalleled importance, and I anchored a-weather to avoid detection." He thought of Madalene and wondered if she was all right. Was she happy? Had she forgot him, already? No. She loved him, she declared as much on the decks of the *Morass* for all to hear. And in a moment of infinite stupidity, he let her go.

"Well, hello, Jean Marc." A blonde with large breasts rubbed against him. "Can I interest you in a blow, or are you in the mood for your usual fare?" She tried to kiss him, but he pulled free, and she whispered in his ear, "I am happy to oblige a windward sail, but it will cost double the regular rate."

The mere suggestion inspired naught but revulsion, as he belonged to Madalene, and he grimaced. "No."

Indeed, Maddie was everywhere and nowhere, at once. As some sort of twisted torment, despite her absence, which he suffered as a gaping wound in his heart, she enveloped him in her presence, claiming his lips, filling his arms, warming his bed in his dreams, and yet when he woke her empty space in his bunk manifested a great chasm threatening to consume him, drive him mad for want of her, or both. If he did not find her soon, there would be hell to pay, as he would tear apart the town until he located his delicate lady and brought her home to the *Morass*.

"Now that is a first." Slapping his thigh, the Iron Corsair tossed a few coins on the table, spread his legs, and unhooked his breeches. "On your knees, and open your mouth, doxy. I will take what he refuses." With a groan, he bared his teeth, as the wench's head bobbed. "So what brings you to Port Royal, as I heard tale of a provisional pardon with England? Let me guess, a woman brings you low?"

"How did you know, as I have said nothing? And the pact with the English is the only means of survival of our kind, and I am responsible for my men. If we are to have a future, we must alter our course, and I have grown weary of looking over my shoulder." Jean Marc stared into his glass and sighed. "What have you learned?"

"There is only one logical conclusion, given you decline the pleasure of a stranger, and I have heard nothing." Barry downed the last of his ale and exhaled audibly. "Ah, that is good." Then he shook his head. "So what is she to you, as I am intrigued?"

"In truth, nothing." Jean Marc revisited her dream and envisioned himself garbed as a gentleman and walking, arm in arm, with Maddie on the streets of Boston. "But she could be everything."

"Then why is she not with you?" The Iron Corsair pounded a clenched fist and grunted. "What did you do?"

"It is a long story, and one I am in no mood to share." Another whore propositioned Jean Marc, and he rejected her advance with a brisk flick of his wrist, as all he wanted was Maddie. "And why are you here?"

"I made the mistake of taking an unfinished job from the Marooner, and it is the last one I will ever assume, but I owed him a debt, and soon it will be repaid." Barry closed his eyes, wrenched the whore's hair, and growled. After securing his breeches, he slapped the doxy on the arse as she stood. "Will you be here, later, darling?"

"I will if you want me to be here." She trailed a finger beneath Barry's chin and winked. "And I will toss whatever you wish."

"Perfect." He waved. "Now be gone with you." To Jean Marc, Barry said, "The Marooner attacked and sank a ship of innocents, all for the sake of a single woman, but the dumb bastard failed to kill his target."

"Oh?" A foreboding chill shivered over Jean Marc's flesh, and panic loomed on the horizon, but he inhaled a deep breath shook off the alarm as a sign of his anxious state. "Anyone we know?"

"I am not sure." The Iron Corsair ordered another ale. "He is secretive with the details, as it is dirty business, and I wish I had never got involved, but I gave him my word, and I will do the deed."

"So I gather." Summoning calm, as he refused to leap to unsupported conclusions, Jean Marc rolled his shoulders. "What did this curious female do to warrant the Marooner's attention?"

"She is an American heiress, or some such." Barry belched and dragged his sleeve across his mouth. "Apparently, her father, an

English lord of ill repute and with a mountain of debt, remarried, and the proverbial stepmother, in anticipation of a blessed event, wants the firstborn gone so that the sire might claim a fortune."

Rage flashed and exploded beneath his flesh, and the desire to kill burned bright as the sun, as Jean Marc lowered his chin and pinned the Iron Corsair with a lethal glare. "Lady Madalene Davies."

"How did you know?" For a few seconds, Barry just sat there. At last, he leaned forward, and his eyes flared. "Do not tell me that is your woman."

"Indeed, and you and I need to talk." Jean Marc propped his elbows on the table. "So I presume the stepmother hired the Marooner to kill Maddie, that the new babe can eventually inherit the estate."

"I am sure she is involved, somehow, as women are always entangled in complicated matters." Barry furrowed his brow and frowned. "But the father paid for the job."

#

Standing at the window overlooking the ocean, Madalene daubed the tears from her face, with a handkerchief, and turned to assess her appearance in the long mirror. Bereft, aching for Jean Marc, she practiced her smile to avoid prying questions, as she could not think of him without succumbing to a deluge of woe. Beneath a contrived mask of cheer, she descended the stairs and joined her father and stepmother in the dining room for an unusually late supper.

"Are you feeling better, Madalene?" Papa toyed with the stem of his crystal glass. "You appeared a bit peaked this morning. Perhaps the sea air does not agree with you."

"On the contrary, I love it here." And Jean Marc would have loved it, too. "In fact, we should set a time to review the planation books and the stillroom ledger, as I noted some discrepancies in the figures, which we should reconcile before ordering additional supplies and services. In the future, I will engage the expertise of an accountant to spare you the responsibility."

"But you may leave that to my care, dear child." He patted the back of her hand. "As such drudgery is not women's work, and I actually enjoy it. Would you not prefer to go shopping with your stepmother? It would give you the opportunity to become better acquainted."

"I would not." In light of Prudence's demeanor, which bordered on downright rude, Madalene made a concerted effort to avoid the ill-mannered woman. "Rather, as I am new to property ownership, I would involve myself in the day to day running of Fair Winds."

"What did I tell you?" Prudence sneered. "She is just arrived and already plans to assume control of Fair Winds."

"You act surprised, stepmother." Folding her arms, Madalene lifted her chin, as she would tolerate no interference from the meddling termagant. "Need I remind you that Fair Winds belonged to my mother's family? And in the Crawford tradition, I intend to assume management of the plantation and its operations."

"I presume you brought Eileen's will and the deed?" Papa asked, and she found his query unnerving and intrusive. "And that reminds me, I had intended to broach the topic tomorrow, but now seems as good a time as any. We should consider having my solicitor draw up terms for a temporary guardianship of the capital, in total, until you take a husband, as the power is too much for a young lady of your limited expertise to handle."

"While I brought certified copies of the original documents, which remain on file with the probate court in Boston, I disagree with your assertion, Papa. Aunt Eileen taught me well, and I shall honor her memory by following in her footsteps." Madalene rested her clasped hands in her lap. "But I put the papers on the desk in the study, as you requested, and we can discuss the situation, tomorrow. The indenture was reissued by a judge, before I departed, to reflect the change in right of possession, and I will not relinquish my authority."

"So everything is in your name?" He reached for his wife and twined his fingers in hers, and Madalene shifted with unease, though she could not explain why. "The bank accounts, the house in Boston, the timber holdings in Virginia, the tobacco farm in Georgia, along with Fair Winds—they are yours? And given you remain unmarried, I am your sole heir?"

"I own it, all, and by law you are my beneficiary." A shiver of dread traipsed her spine, and she did not understand why she viewed him as a threat, given he was her father.

"And you intend to preside over the estate, in its entirety?" Papa arched a brow. "You cannot be persuaded otherwise?"

"As Aunt Eileen expected, I will assume direction of the assets." To her amazement,

Papa actually glowered. "Is that a problem?"

"It is for you." He waved, and she glanced behind her.

A group of menacing characters, dirty and disheveled, similar to the crew who sailed the *Black Morass*, entered the dining room. Assuming stations at either side of her, they appeared bent on mischief, and Madalene peered at her sire.

"What is going on, Papa?" Shivering, she clamped her jaw to conceal her trembling, and it was too late when she realized the significance of their awkward and tense conversation. "Who are these men?"

"Your new masters, my dear." In that instant, Papa dipped his chin, and the men closed in on her. "You will begin your life with them, as I have fixed a date with the magistrate, to have you declared dead and to undertake proprietorship of the Crawford fortune. I do thank you for bringing me the necessary documents to enact my scheme."

"How could you do this?" As she endured the second heartbreak in three days, she swallowed hard. "We are only recently reunited, and I am your daughter, your blood."

"But I never wanted a daughter, as I require a son to carry on my name and title."

He sneered with unmasked contempt. "And my interest in you extended only insofar as you possessed the means by which I could seize the Crawford fortune. Beyond that, I care naught for you."

"You will never succeed." Crushed by his indifference and unimaginable cruelty, she pushed from the table, stood, and her chair toppled to the floor. To a pirate, she said, "Do not touch me, sir."

"Now, now." The tall, clean-shaven brute reminded her of Jean Marc, if not for the blonde hair and the missing scar and patch, and he wagged a finger in reproach. "Do not fight, dove, as you will lose, and my partner will not abide damaged merchandise."

"Take her." Papa drew Prudence to his side, and Madalene realized she had been duped by a stranger she never should have trusted. "But you should demand a steep price, as she comes from prime stock."

With that, Madalene faced a full-scale assault, as an assailant gagged her with a long kerchief, while another bound her wrists. And even amid the shocking attack, as terror waged war with her senses, Jean Marc occupied her thoughts. If only he knew of her distress, he would save her. Perhaps she could bargain with her captor, as her bawdy buccaneer would rescue her, if he knew of her plight. At least, that was what she told herself, as the pirates dragged her into the hall, and she moaned and kicked in protest.

"Easy, *Mon Chou*." The leader laughed. "I know someone eager to make your acquaintance, so let us not delay."

It dawned on her in that single fragment in time, when a familiar address chipped through the chill of horror and shook her to attention, that the situation was not so grievous as it seemed. The scoundrel called her by Jean Marc's favored term of endearment, and she knew, without doubt, her man had come for her. Somewhere, in the dark of night, he waited. At least, she prayed he waited, as she could not bear to think otherwise.

So she ceased her opposition, yielded to her captors, and strolled to a group of horses in the drive. Despite instincts to the contrary, she resisted not when her primary subduer thrust her atop his mount, leaped into the saddle, heeled the flanks of the stallion, and set a blazing pace. When the motley crew passed beneath the Fair Winds sign, she bade farewell to her brief home, as she knew not whether she would ever see it again.

Fighting the urge to rebel, she accepted her fear and resolved to meet her fate, whatever it might be, with grace and courage. She knew not how far they traveled, but the journey seemed endless, as she marked the moon's path in the sky. At long last, they navigated a sandy dune, and she spied torchlight ahead. When her detainer reined in and jumped to the ground, she scanned the vicinity for some sign of Jean Marc.

Instead, the fair-haired rogue yanked her down, brandished a knife, and cut the ropes from her wrists. In seconds, she wrenched free of the gag and inhaled a deep breath. Just as she was about to voice a complaint, she spied Tyne amid a group on the beach and bolted in his direction. As she neared, the men parted.

Splaying wide his arms, Jean Marc flicked his fingers. "It is good see you, *Mon Chou*, as I have missed you."

How many nights had he come to her in her dreams, only to disappoint her when she woke the next morning? Only two, but it was two too many. Fear mixed with anger and found a convenient outlet, as she slapped him hard.

CHAPTER TEN

Prepared for all manner of feminine hysterics, Jean Marc did not anticipate a wicked blow to his cheek, but his lady continued to impress him with her prowess. Neither did he expect the ensuing pummeling, as Maddie unleashed her ire and aggression, mingling punches and kicks with various inventive curses, and he would have laughed had he not been the cause of her anguish. In light of her usual serene and elegant demeanor, her expression of fury wounded him. In seconds, his crew vacated the immediate vicinity, and he considered halting her tantrum.

Instead, he stood there and took her anger, as it was nothing less than he deserved.

After a few minutes, she collapsed against his chest and clung to him, and he held her tight. "Shh, *Mon Chou*. It is all right. You were never in danger."

"How could you abandon me?" Crying openly, she wrenched his shirt. "How could you let go, after everything we shared?" She shoved him. "Am I nothing to you? Do you not care?"

"Do you see me here? Look at me, Maddie." Grasping the hair at the nape of her neck, he forced her to meet his stare, and she sobbed. "I did not abandon you." Ever so briefly, he pressed his lips to hers. "I never departed Port Royal, because I could not bear to leave you. And it is not out of some misplaced, proprietary sense that you belong to me, although I submit you are mine, but because I am yours. Because I belong to you, whether in Port Royal or in Boston. The *Morass* is anchored offshore, where she has been for the past three days." Then he kissed her hard, and he gave her no quarter until she softened. "When I discovered your father's plan, and his motivation, I made a deal with the devil to save you, because I cannot live without you."

"Am I so special, as I had not noticed. And Papa wants the Fair Winds." She sniffed and nuzzled his chest. "He wants everything for his unborn babe, and he never wanted to know me. It was all a cruel trick to lure me here, so he could commission my death." With a whimper, which gnawed at his gut, she returned his kiss. "I am a fool, Jean Marc. I believed in you, and you rejected me. I trusted my father, and he sold me to the highest bidder. Does no one want me?"

"No, *Mon Chou*, you are no fool, and I was wrong to let go. You are a benevolent angel, and you are my salvation. But your father is an English bastard with debts as large as his pride." With his sleeve, he dried her cheeks and claimed another kiss. "But it will be all right, as I have a solution that will provide protection and set you free."

"How?" She inhaled a shivery breath. "As long as I am alive, I am a threat to his inheritance, as I am the rightful owner of the Crawford estate, and my father is my beneficiary, a fact he knows too well. He will stop at nothing to win the money, and he will never let me live in peace."

"Yet, there is a way to outsmart him, if you are willing to listen to reason and consider a different path, with me." Jean Marc trailed the pad of his thumb along the curve of her jaw and then caressed her lower lip. "What if you had another beneficiary, one whose rights superseded your sire's?" At her countenance of confusion, he explained, "Your father could not prevail over the lawful authority of your husband."

"You want to marry me for the endowment?" The hurt in her expression tore at his heart.

"No, *Mon Chou*." Framing her face, he summoned pretty words and phrases, trying to find the right appeal, so she would understand what she meant to him. In the end, he settled on the truth. "I do not give a damn about your bloody legacy, as I have no need of your riches. But I love your dream, almost as much as I love you. That is why I would make you my wife, so I can guard and defend you. So I can live out my days with you at my side, content in the knowledge that you are legally required to be there, as the nights are an eternity without you in my bunk. What say you, Maddie?"

"Proposals are usually made on bended knee." She pouted, yanked on his leather thong, and released it, such that it smacked his forehead. "And take off that infernal eye patch, as you know I detest it."

In that instant, he laughed. "Oh, how I missed you, my fiery society lady." Glancing over his shoulder, he prepared for the hailstorm of jokes at his expense, but he would do anything for Maddie, so he knelt before her, took her hand in his, and pulled a bauble from his pocket. "So you have me where you want me, *Mon Chou*. I am yours to command, as I am the man who loves you. I want nothing more than to share your dream and ride your beautiful round arse, until the day I die. What say you, Maddie? Will you marry me?"

"Well, that is not the most romantic proposal I have ever heard, but I suppose it will have to do." Then she pounced on him. "*Yes*." Showering him in sweet kisses, she giggled. "Yes, yes, a thousand times, yes."

#

Beneath the silvery moonlight and a blanket of stars, and amid the audial tapestry of the incoming tide, the beachside wedding featured a cluster of tropical blooms as a hasty, improvised bouquet, and the groom sported black leather breeches and a flowing white linen shirt, his customary attire, along with two pistols tucked in his waistband, but she pretended not to notice. Surrounded by the surliest, most well-fortified bridal party in history, battle-hardened creatures bearing countless knives and swords, Lady Madalene Davies stood beside ex-pirate Jean Marc Cavalier, as a stodgy and proper parson read from the Book of Common Prayer. With Tyne acting as best man and maid of honor, it was an interesting contradiction, to say the least.

Focusing on the vows, she faced her soon-to-be spouse, held his hands, and pledged, "My heart will be your shelter, and my arms will be your home."

Then it was her buccaneer's turn, and he infused his words with various inflections she understood too well. Never had she found anything sacred so humorous, as Jean Marc waggled his brows.

The parson closed the tome and cleared his throat. "By the power invested in me, I now pronounce you husband and wife. Mr. Cavalier, you may kiss your bride."

Just as she anticipated, her marauder swept her into his embrace and favored her with a thorough expression of his ardor, which set the tone for their union, and she encouraged him with additional flicks and darts of her tongue.

When they surfaced, she gasped. "Where did you find an honest man of the cloth to perform the ceremony, or is it not legal?"

"*Mon Chou*, for good or ill, you are mine by law." The barbarian raider surfaced with a snicker. "And Mr. Boone's parsonage requires a new roof, which I was only too happy to pay for, in exchange for his services."

"How resourceful is my husband." She squealed when he bent and hoisted her over his shoulder. "Oh, Jean Marc, what are you doing?"

"It is time to seal our promise in the customary fashion." In a few strides, he carried her to the jolly boat, where the pirate leader who took her from the Fair Winds lingered. "Maddie, meet the Iron Corsair. He conspired to help me liberate you from your bastard father, and now I am in Barry's debt, which is never good."

"A pleasure to make your acquaintance." From her odd perch, she extended her hand, and the rogue winked and pressed his lips to the back of her knuckles, as if the sight of Jean Marc carrying a woman in that manner was an every day occurrence. "But you really should have given me some indication of my husband's involvement in your scheme, as you gave me a terrible fright."

"The pleasure is mine, Mrs. Cavalier, and I

apologize if I scared you, but I needed to maintain the ruse, should your father have posted spies along the route." He clucked his tongue. "But my efforts were worth it, as I never thought I would see the day that Jean Marc took a bride, yet stranger things have happened."

"Enough talk." Jean Marc deposited her on the middle bench in the tiny craft and then eased behind her, so that she perched between his legs, as when he taught her to fish. "Now make yourself useful and give us a heave-ho."

With a loud whistle, the Iron Corsair summoned the crew, and amid ribald well wishes and questionable congratulations, the men pushed the small skiff into the tide, whereupon they drifted on the current. As her husband rowed them to the *Morass*, she rested against his chest and caressed his thighs.

In exchange, he licked and suckled the sensitive flesh at the base of her ear, and his breath grew ragged, when she took his hand and pressed it to her breast. She needed no warning to know their coupling would be neither gentle nor quick, as the rock-hard erection resting against her derriere beckoned, even then. But she wanted no gentleness from her husband.

At the mainsail hull, he held steady the Jacob's ladder, as she climbed to the waist. When he joined her, he swept her off her feet and kissed her, as he navigated the lower deck of the ship.

"Where is everyone?" She noted the eerie quiet of the usually bustling and noisy vessel.

"They will sleep ashore, tonight." In his cabin, he slammed shut the door and threw her none-too-softly on the bunk. After stripping off his shirt, he doffed his boots and breeches and turned his attention to her garments. Naked and aroused, he pleasured himself and smiled. "And now that I have spoken the vows, I am bloody well going to enjoy the consummation."

And so it commenced.

Spearing his fingers in her hair, he led her to his chair, where he sat, spread his legs, brought her to her knees, and took her mouth. For the next few hours, he bent her over the washstand and claimed her bottom, pinned her against the wall and sailed her honey harbor, rolled her on the bunk, until they fell to the boards, and started all over again at the little table where they took their meals.

Given the emotional events of the day,

Madalene heeled his flanks, taunted him with her body, slapped his arse, and spurred his base desires, if only to remind herself that he was with her. And he was hers.

By the time they collapsed on the mattress, spent and sated, there were no more secrets or fears between them. Indeed, they were one entity, ready to face the future and all its uncertainty.

"Are you hungry, *Mon Chou*?" Jean Marc stroked her hair and kissed her forehead. "I can fetch us something from the galley, and then you should rest, as we cast off in the morning."

"Where are we going?" She sat upright.

"Wherever we want." He shrugged. "The world is ours, my wife. You need only name the destination."

For a few minutes, she pondered the day's events and her father's dastardly plan to steal the Crawford estate, and an idea formed in her brain. "My cherished husband, I am famished, and I will eat whatever you can manage. But as to your proposal, thank you, but no. We are not leaving.

CHAPTER ELEVEN

"This hearing shall come to order." A bailiff dressed in a peacock uniform and a powdered wig hammered the floor with the friendly end of what appeared to be some sort of medieval battle-axe, in the main courthouse in Port Royal. "Please rise for the Honorable Judge John Abrams."

The attendees stood.

The repetitive hammer of the gavel brought the proceeding to order, and Madalene's father loomed beside his solicitor as the jurist read several documents.

"We have come here, today, to discuss the petition by Lord Nigel Davies, Earl of

Livingston, to declare his daughter, Lady Madalene Davies, missing and presumed deceased. And in the matter of the Fair Winds plantation, as well as Lady Madalene's estate, I hold an order for probate and immediate transfer of all assets into Lord Livingston's care, custody, and control." The judge removed his spectacles and wrinkled his nose. "Are there any witnesses present to provide into evidence any reason why I should not forthwith grant Lord Livingston's request?"

"I shall swear testimony to that effect." In a proud moment he would never forget, Jean Marc trailed in Maddie's wake, as she charged the bench, along with a solicitor, Mr. Holcomb, she engaged to represent her cause.

"And who would you be?" Judge Abrams inquired.

His haughty society miss, gowned in one of her dainty, lace-collared confections, thrust her chin. "Lady Madalene Davies."

And all hell broke loose.

With fingers pointing in every direction, and accusations flying, the judge convened a small gathering of the interested parties and their attorneys, to which Jean Marc was not invited.

Pacing in the courtroom, he laughed as

Livingston's voice reverberated from the inner chamber, and he scowled at Lady Prudence, who also remained in the gallery. Then four redcoats entered from the rear, and Jean Marc tugged at his collar. When the soldiers assumed positions at either side of him, he nodded once and smiled.

After almost half an hour, the parties emerged, and Maddie's glow declared her victory. "My love, it is too wonderful. While Papa thought he won the day, the judge reviewed the parcel of documents I brought from Boston, which bore my signature, as certified by the American probate court. To prove my identity, Judge Abrams bade me sign my name, which I did, and of course it matched, perfectly. But I must write my attorney at home, for additional support, and Father has been given a month to prove his case."

"That is wonderful, *Mon Chou.*" He tucked a stray tendril behind her ear and noted the approaching guards. "So, what is next?"

"Judge Abrams issued a subpoena for the testimony of Lieutenant Lowe, as my father gave no impression that I was anyone other than I claimed, when the soldier delivered me to Fair Winds." Maddie rocked on her heels. "Despite my father's dastardly machinations, I shall prevail, my love."

The judge brought the courtroom to attention and cleared his throat. "Given some discrepancies in Lord Livingston's petition, I shall defer any final ruling pending an appeal. Lord Livingston may maintain the residence hereby designated as the Fair Winds Plantation, until such time as he has exhausted all appeals. And the party identified as Lady Madalene Davies shall produce, in two month's time, additional verification of rightful ownership of said property. The other holdings in the Crawford estate shall remain in their current state, bound to the listed possessor of record, owing to the outcome of these pended cases." Then Judge Abrams pinned Jean Marc with an icy glare. "It has come to this court's attention that the criminal known as Jean Marc Cavalier, forthwith known as the defendant, is present. I hereby direct the bailiff to take the defendant into custody, to be charged for crimes against the Crown."

#

Madalene almost fainted.

When they traveled to the courthouse that day, all she thought about was her inheritance and besting her father and Lady Prudence. Never did Maddie consider the threat to Jean

Marc, given his history. How could she have been so blind?

"Have Tyne take you back to Boston, as it is over for us, *Mon Chou*." After Jean Marc calmly kissed her, he faced the advancing soldiers and held out his hands. "Gentlemen, I have no wish to cause any trouble. Indeed, I surrender into your safekeeping."

"No." When she tried to reach her husband, a redcoat stepped in her path. "You are mistaken. He has changed." In a panic, she attempted to shove the soldier, but he stood his ground, as Jean Marc was led away. "Please." She approached the bench. "Judge Abrams, my husband is a good and decent man. I know he made mistakes in the past, but he is no longer a pirate."

"Be that as it may, the defendant owes a debt to society, and it must be paid." The judge pushed from his chair and frowned. "I recommend you retain the services of your solicitor, as your husband will need representation."

"Wait." In blind desperation, she grabbed his arm. "I beg you, a word, sir. There are extenuating circumstances that I am not at liberty to share in public."

"I have no time to waste, Lady Madalene." He shifted his weight. "You will tell me, here and now, else we are done."

Given her father and Lady Prudence lingered, Madalene bent and whispered in the judge's ear, and he gasped in surprise. "As a servant of the Crown, you must acknowledge my husband's newfound status, sir. Pray, give me ample opportunity to gather proof of what I say and witnesses to speak on Jean Marc's behalf. If necessary, I will gladly relinquish all claims to the Crawford estate and sail from Port Royal with my husband, on pain of never returning to Jamaica."

"If you speak the truth, then I am compelled to do so, and there is no need to make such a sacrifice, as the matters are separate." Judge Abrams furrowed his brow and appeared to consider her plea. "In light of the requisite travel associated with your claim, you have two months, Lady Madalene."

"Thank you." Relieved to a degree, she clutched her hands to her bosom. "Thank you, so much."

And then she dashed outside, as she had not a moment to spare. At the road, she glanced left and then right. Lurking beneath a shade tree, Tyne chuckled and slapped a member of the crew on the back. When the first mate spotted her, he lurched upright.

"What is it, Madalene?" He peered over

her shoulder. "And where is Jean Marc?"

"He has been arrested." She swallowed hard. "And I need you to take me to the *Black Morass*."

CHAPTER TWELVE

"Cavalier, you are commanded to appear before the magistrate." A redcoat unlocked the cell, and the door creaked and groaned in protest, as he set wide the bars. "If you will follow me, you are to bathe, shave, and dress for the appointment."

Since Jean Marc did not think the English washed and cleaned their convicts before they hung them, he supposed it was the final meeting, whereupon he would be sentenced for his crimes. Resolved to meet his date with destiny in the spirit in which he lived, he did as his jailer bade.

To his surprise, he found a pair of black

leather breeches and a white linen shirt draped on a chair, and new boots, polished to perfection, rested near the hearth. By the razor on the washstand, he located a thong, which he used to pull back his hair, as he groomed. Looking more like himself, he lingered by a window and gazed at the yard, where prisoners took their exercise, and wondered if he would ever hold Maddie in his arms again.

In the two months since his arrest, her visits were limited to a few short conversations through the bars of his confinement, and it was the separation that tormented him most, as he longed for her warmth. But in the solitude of his captivity, he realized he had to prepare her for the worst, as it was his responsibility as her husband.

Husband.

Now that was a word he had never understood. Comprised of seven simple, nondescript letters when considered on their own, but taken together as a whole, they formed the single most important oath he could make, and he vowed he would not fail his wife. It was his duty to ensure Maddie's future, and he had to be strong for her sake.

He had committed some horrible deeds in

his lifetime, and the ferryman called for his due. If he had known what fate had in store for him, that he would happen upon a beautiful society miss in distress, and she would rescue him, in every way possible, he would have tried harder to redeem himself. But it was too late to undo the crimes of his youthful ignorance and adult vengeance.

"Are you ready, Cavalier?" The soldier stood at attention.

"Aye." He nodded once and steeled himself. "Let us get on with it."

A narrow passage led to the processing room, where the redcoat paused to sign a document.

"Hold out your hands." A jailer shackled Jean Marc.

Exiting beneath a portico, which shielded the sunlight from his sensitive eyes, he noted a black carriage with iron bars on the windows. Following his escort's directions, Jean Marc climbed into the rig, which conveyed him and the lobster to the courthouse. Waiting on the stairs in the front of the building, along with Mr. Holcomb, Maddie bounced and waved. When Jean Marc disembarked, she framed his face and kissed him.

"Oh, my love, it is so good to see you."

Then she noted the iron manacles, frowned, and cast a wicked glare at the soldier. "Is this necessary, as my husband is going nowhere without me?"

"Afraid so, until the judge declares otherwise, ma'am." The redcoat clutched Jean Marc by the elbow. "Let us go inside."

In the courtroom, the judge spoke with two gentlemen, one of whom Jean Marc recognized, and he wondered if he dreamed the whole affair. "What is Sir Ross Logan doing here?"

"Shh." Maddie held a finger to her lips. "Sit down, and smile, as I would rather you not seem so menacing, and Sir Ross has come to our aid."

The proceedings continued for several minutes, and Logan gestured wildly on a couple of occasions. Every now and then, the judge peered at Jean Marc, and he adopted his best pose, in obeisance of Maddie's pedestrian request. But how did a swashbuckling buccaneer who had committed numerous egregious crimes assume an air of cherubic innocence? Then Sir Ross strolled past Jean Marc and sat beside Madalene.

"Let us come to order." The judge pounded his gavel, removed his spectacles, and steepled his hands. "In light of recent evidence in support of the former pirate known as Jean Marc Cavalier, hereafter referred to as the defendant, it is the court's opinion that the defendant should be set free to continue the terms of the pact sworn by an agent of His Majesty, with the understanding that any future crimes committed will not be subject to the terms of the pardon, and the defendant shall be remanded into custody to be tried under the law, as would any citizen. The defendant is free to go."

In that moment, Maddie squealed with unabashed delight, and he turned directly into her arms. "Thank you, *Mon Chou.*" Then Jean Marc extended a hand in friendship. "And I owe you a debt, Sir Ross. But how did you know I was in trouble?"

"You must be joking." Logan laughed. "It appears you married a woman every bit as strong-willed as mine, and I am not sure whether to congratulate or pity you." To Maddie, Ross said, "And you can stop writing to the Crown Court, the Ambassador, the King, and anyone else you were badgering, as your husband is liberated."

"Thank you, so much, for helping us, although I did not give you much choice." She bit her bottom lip. "And the accord remains in effect?"

"It does." Ross gathered his papers. "But I encourage you to maintain a low profile until you successfully complete the terms of the agreement."

"That is not a problem." Maddie peered at Jean Marc, and he noted a telltale spark of fire. "As I intend to keep him occupied and out of mischief."

He liked the sound of that.

"How is Lady Elaine?" Jean Marc inquired.

"I am pleased to report she is with child." Ross rolled his eyes. "But she spends most mornings with her head in a basin, and it was all I could do to depart London without her, as she begged to come with me. Yet, I wager she will meet you in the Atlantic when the year is ended, to celebrate your triumph, as that is one battle I know I will not win, and she is dying to form an acquaintance with your bride."

"Will you give her our regards?" Maddie sidled close to Jean Marc, and he wrapped his arm about her waist. "And I am equally anxious to make her acquaintance."

"I will do so." Ross slapped Jean Marc on the shoulder. "Now, if you do not mind, I have a ship to catch, as I would return home with all due haste, and I am sure you can understand."

"Indeed, I do, as there is something that requires my attention, and I aim to be about it." Slowly, he skimmed his palm to his wife's hip, and she tensed. Ah, she was just as hungry. "Shall we depart for the *Morass, Mon Chou?*"

"Actually, I have taken a room in a hotel, as we cannot leave just yet." Grasping his wrist, she dragged him to her carriage. "My father is to vacate the Fair Winds in a sennight, as he has exhausted all appeals. And the judge ordered Papa to return to England, an arrival his creditors anticipate with baited breath, so I presume. Thus I would ensure neither he nor that wench he married take anything that is not theirs. It is bad enough Lady Prudence stole Mama's cameo, and I fear I shall never see it again. Given my hasty departure, against my will, the last time I dined there, I have no idea what became of my personal belongings, which remained in my room at the plantation house."

"You will get them back." He made a mental note to arrange a midnight raid, as he settled into the squabs. "So what shall we do in the meantime?"

Maddie lowered the shades and perched in his lap. Pressing her lips to his, she sighed. "Perhaps I can inspire you."

#

By the time they reached the room at the hotel, Maddie was ready to burst. When Jean Marc engaged the lock, she kicked off her slippers, hiked her skirts and chemise, bared her bottom, and bent over the footboard of the large bed.

"I wore the hose with the little blue bows, just for you, my love." And then she waited.

Laughing, he gave her a playful smack. "How I missed this sight, *Mon Chou*." Then, to her surprise, he pulled her upright and tugged at her laces. "While you tempt me with your succulent arse, there is something else I prefer, just now." In minutes, he stripped her bare of any clothing, and he pulled the pins from her coif, letting her long brown hair spill about her shoulders. "You have put on some weight, my dear, and I like it."

"Well, I would not get used to it, as it is temporary." There was so much she wanted to share with him. So much she needed to say, yet the right phrasing eluded her.

"What do you mean it is temporary?" He snorted. "Do you intend to reduce, as you are beautiful, Maddie?"

"Actually, I will increase before I lose anything." She swallowed hard. "But the period is relatively short, in the grand scheme." She shrugged. "You know, the usual nine months?" He sobered and opened his mouth but quickly clamped it shut, and she wrenched his shirt. "Tell me you are happy, as I desperately need to hear it."

"*Mon Chou*, in truth, there are no words to adequately describe what I feel right now, so I suppose happy must do." He kissed her softly, inexpressibly sweet, as he framed her face. "I love you, Maddie."

In that instant, she collapsed in a fit of tears. "Oh, Jean Marc, I am so sorry I put my family's estate before you. If we had departed Port Royal, as you wanted, none of this would have happened. Your incarceration was all my fault, and I beg your forgiveness."

"No, you are blameless." Setting her apart, he ripped off his clothes and boots and then drew her into his embrace. "I committed those crimes long before I ever met you, and I, alone, must atone for them."

"Then you are not vexed with me?" She held her breath, as she needed his forgiveness.

"No, *Mon Chou*." Again, he kissed her. "Never could I be angry with you, when you saved me."

Confused, she searched her mind but could not discern his meaning. "But—how?"

"I would not have made it this far, had we not met." He led her to the bed and pushed onto her back. In seconds he covered her. Nose to nose, he teased her flesh. "But you shared your dream, and somewhere on our journey to Port Royal, your fantasy became mine. I want more, and I want it with you." With his legs, he spread wide her thighs. "Enough talk, and I will ride your pretty arse tomorrow. Right now, I want to make love to my wife."

CHAPTER THIRTEEN

In the wee hours, Jean Marc kissed Maddie's forehead and then withdrew from her arms. Since adjourning to bed, it had taken three rounds of rigorous coitus to satisfy her and put her to sleep, so he could enact his hastily sketched plan. Given the revelation of his impending fatherhood, he had to act on his wife and his unborn babe's behalf.

It was a rare thing to care for someone, to know that Maddie's happiness depended on Jean Marc's ability to keep the smile on her beautiful face. In his lifetime, he had confronted every manner of evil, yet nothing scared him more than the powerful but delicate bonds of love and the chance that he might fail her. The commitment he made, the most important of his existence, defined him in ways he could not have foreseen, and a consuming desire to protect Maddie drove him into the throes of an unquenchable thirst for violence. To his amazement, he struggled with an insatiable bloodlust. In order to guarantee his wife's future, he had to delve into his brutal past and summon the beast.

As he tugged on his breeches and boots, she shifted and sniffed, and he held still until she quieted. In the dark, he fumbled for his weapons, collected his pistols and dagger, and pulled on his shirt. After searching his trunk, in the dark, he located the item his wife found so offensive, because she claimed it gave him an air of menace—and that suited his purpose.

Stretching upright, he donned the familiar black patch behind which Maddie argued he hid his true persona, and she could not have been more correct in her assertion, as only his highborn wife glimpsed the side he concealed from the public. But that night he required the ill repute of the meanest, most villainous pirate to sail the seas.

When his lady mumbled, he grabbed an extra blanket from the footboard, draped the swath of wool over her form, and tucked the cover beneath her chin, to keep her warm until he returned. Responsibility for another offered a new and unsettling experience he did not quite savor, as husbandly duty brought with it a palpable fear when he pondered Madalene's fate should he disappoint her—but he would not founder. After a final check to ensure her comfort, he stole another kiss and slipped from their room.

Posted in the hall, two of his men remained on watch.

"Cap'n." Boyle came alert. "We did not expect to see you until morning."

"Or afternoon." Riggs elbowed the tar, and they laughed.

"Wake Tyne, and fetch the six best riders in the crew." To Boyle, Jean Marc said, "Guard Maddie with your life, and no one is permitted to disturb her. If I am not back by dawn, take her to the *Morass* and set sail for Boston."

"Aye, sir." The sailor nodded.

Downstairs, he gathered his band of buccaneers for one last raid.

"My friends, my wife is with child, and her sire presents a very real threat to her safety, which I cannot ignore." As the sea dogs offered congratulations, Jean Marc paused to collect his thoughts. "What I ask of you is dangerous."

"What is new about that?" Tyne snickered. "And I knew of your good news, given I fetched the doctor, but your delicate bride vowed in a not-so-delicate manner to cut off my Jolly Roger if I told you."

The men guffawed.

"All right." Jean Marc silenced his men with a sweep of his hand. "Given her condition, I cannot let Lord Livingston's attempts to kill Maddie go unanswered."

"Cap'n is right." Tyne chucked Jean Marc's shoulder. "Lady Madalene is one of us, and Livingston's attack demands a response."

"Let us pay a visit to the plantation." Randall smacked a fist to a palm. "We will teach that arrogant English bastard a lesson he will not soon forget."

"Then we ride." Jean Marc waved a pistol, and the sailors cheered.

Outside, they gained their mounts and set a course for the outskirts of Port Royal. The journey, an endless torture comprised of hideous visions of Maddie in her father's charge, plagued Jean Marc, and he was grateful when the sun-washed gate of the Fair Winds came into view.

In the trees that lined the grand drive, they

secured their horses and skulked to the main house. As a cool breeze drifted from the ocean, most of the windows had been shut and latched, but he made entry via an unlocked terrace door.

The floorboards creaked beneath his feet, as he inched into the residence. In the dark, he reached with outstretched hands and skimmed the wall with his fingers. A hallway led to the rear of the home, and based on Maddie's description, he sought the chamber she briefly occupied and collected her bag of keepsakes, which remained where she left them.

At the end of the passage, he turned the knob of the double-door portal and signaled his crew. On the count of three, which he whispered, they rushed their prey. Surrounding the sleeping couple, the men grabbed Livingston and his young bride.

"Make no sound, Lord Livingston." Jean Marc lit a bedside taper and then stretched across the foot of the mattress. "If you scream, you die." To Randall, Jean Marc commanded, "Gag and bind the lady, as I have no patience for her."

When Livingston moaned in protest, Tyne slapped the nobleman on the side of the head. "Shut up, as you are lucky that is all we will do to her."

And then silence fell on the master suite.

"That was a cunning maneuver you devised, hiring a pirate to kill your daughter, making her appear a hapless victim of high seas treachery, so you could inherit the fortune bequeathed to her, by a family you considered beneath your estimable English heritage." Jean Marc drew his dagger from the waistband of his breeches and toyed with the blade. "How many casualties did you deem acceptable to accomplish your goal, so you could line your pockets with money you neither earned nor deserved?" He arched a brow. "Fifty or sixty innocents?"

Tyne snickered. "And they call us callous blackguards."

The pampered scoundrel shook his head.

"I should kill you," Jean Marc declared, in a low tone.

Wide-eyed, Livingston groaned.

"But Maddie would not like that, so I shall spare you." With the knife, Jean Marc pointed for emphasis. "However, your fate is predicated on Madalene's survival. Should she slip and fall on her tea, should she drown in her bath, should she suffer mortal injuries from an accidental collision with a runaway carriage, or should she meet some strange and unexplainable misfortune, *you will die.*"

Again, the aristocrat protested.

"But you will not meet your demise by my hand—at least, not directly." Now Jean Marc sat upright, as the time for polite pleasantries had ended. "Oh, no, as that is too easy. First, I will give you and your fetching bride to my men, as some prefer ladies, while others enjoy the unutterable defilement of the firm male arse, particularly a pale, highborn English bottom. At my discretion, they will use you, until your back breaks from the strain, and then I will cut you, for sport, because I want you alive when I toss you into the sea, that you may suffer when the sharks take the first bite of your flesh. So you had better pray your daughter is blessed with a long and healthy life, thus I have no reason to call upon you." He shifted, crawled to Maddie's father, and perched nose to nose with the spoiled sot. "Do we understand each other, Lord Livingston?"

Livingston nodded.

"Excellent." Jean Marc glanced at Tyne. "See? I told you the English were a sensible lot." Leaping from the mattress, he snapped his fingers. "Now where is Maddie's cameo, as I will not leave without it?"

After a quick peek at the lady, Lord

Livingston responded, "In the jewelry box on my wife's vanity."

In seconds, Jean Marc located the item, which he secured in his pocket, and then he sketched a bow. "Lord Livingston, it was a pleasure."

With the nasty bit of business behind him, Jean Marc led his men back to their mounts, and they set a course for town. It was a quiet ride in the solitude of twilight, and during that time he considered his unborn babe.

At an imaginary crossroads, he had a decision to make, the outcome of which would impact not only Maddie but also his heir. In a moment of stark clarity, he realized he was past due for a change. He wanted to attend the birth of his child, to teach him to fish, to respect women, and to earn an honest living. More than that, he wanted to grow old with Maddie, to sit on a porch in a creaky wooden rocker and watch the leaves turn and fall. And he could not do that as captain of the *Black Morass*. In that moment, he doffed the black patch and tossed it alongside the road.

So he would start anew, in more ways than one.

After securing the horses and his crew, Jean Marc tiptoed, yes, he bloody well tiptoed, into the room he shared with his wife. In seconds, he stripped naked and joined her beneath the covers. Almost immediately, she turned into him, inched near, kissed his chest, and sighed.

"Is something wrong, my love?" She sniffled.

"No, *Mon Chou*." Wrapping his arms about her, he pulled her closer into his protective embrace.

As he settled in the down mattress, the bone weariness of the past couple of months abated, and he found comfort in the steady beat of her heart and her rhythmic exhalations, which slowed their accompaniment as she returned to the land of dreams. For a long while, he rubbed his lips to her forehead, savoring the warmth that was uniquely Maddie's, reassuring himself that she remained very much alive and well and would persist at his side for the rest of his days. At last, Jean Marc smiled to himself and slept.

#

The subtle sashay of warm lips to the crest of her ear brought Madalene awake, as she rested on her side. Yawning, she stretched long on the blanket, as Jean Marc trailed a series of kisses along the curve of her neck.

"Do not tell me it is time to return to the ship." Opening her eyes, she blinked and then admired the calm surface of the little cove, her favorite place, and smiled. "It is still light, so we can indulge in another swim."

"I thought you were in a hurry to arrive home, and at this rate, it could take another fortnight to make Boston." With care, he spread her bottom cheeks, withdrew his length from her body, and then pulled her to recline on her back. After a vast deal more than thorough kiss, which stirred her in an altogether different manner, he nipped the tip of her nose and caressed her bare breast. "I love you, Maddie."

"And I you, my love." As usual, when she invoked the term of endearment, he blushed, and she adored him for it. Naked, she giggled, rolled free, leaped to her feet, and ran into the water, with her equally nude husband on her heels. "You cannot catch me."

"Oh, I believe we both know I will, and I will have my way with you, when I do, *Mon Chou.*" With a wicked grin, he dove into the blue depths, and she followed suit.

Together, they engaged in a graceful ballet, of sorts, legs twining, arms reaching, hands groping, mouths merging in a communion of souls, until they broke for air.

With her arms and legs wrapped tight about her husband, she grazed her teeth to his chin. "Please, I want you."

In silence, he cupped her derriere, carried her to the blanket on the beach, knelt, and pushed her down. And so his voluptuous assault commenced, as he rode her hard and fast, just as she liked it, until he collapsed, spent and sated, atop her. Then the true coupling began, as Jean Marc loved her with his lips on hers and caressed her face. He whispered sweet praise and told her what she did to him, how she made him feel, and it was in those tender moments that she knew, without a shadow of a doubt, she was right where she belonged.

Since departing Port Royal, the tenor of his passion had changed. While the intensity of their lovemaking had not waned, how he achieved the heights of desire now relied less upon physical aggression and more upon the invisible connections unrestrained by the mortal shell. And the devotion Maddie thought had reached the limits of its breadth grew beyond her wildest expectations. The resulting ties bound her to her bawdy buccaneer, such that she knew not where he began and she ended.

No, Jean Marc was not what she expected when she envisioned her future husband, as she supposed she would happen upon a proper gentleman, favor his profile, and wed. But never had she considered her father would conspire to kill her for the Crawford fortune, that she would be left for dead in the middle of the ocean, and her survival would rely upon the courage and honor of a once ruthless pirate.

"The hour grows late, and we should depart for the *Morass*." Sitting upright, Jean Marc furrowed his brow and appeared lost in thought. "You know, I am considering a name change for my ship, to reflect my new occupation as a gentleman merchant."

"But the current one suits its captain, given his predilections." She stuck her tongue in her cheek.

With a countenance of confusion, he scratched his chin. "I do not understand."

"Never mind." She laughed. "But before we leave our private paradise, will you fetch the ledger from the sack, as there is something I wish to show you?"

"All right, but we cannot linger, as we must trudge through the jungle, and I will not risk injury to you." He snapped his fingers after collecting the register. "Actually, I believe I should carry you and avoid the danger, altogether."

"Whatever you wish, my love." She

nodded once. "Now open the book, as it contains papers that specifically relate to you, and I would have you aware of the arrangements I made on your behalf, to ensure your well-being, should something happen to me."

"*My* well-being?" His expression sobered, and he set aside the ledger, folded his legs, and pulled her into his lap. "*Mon Chou*, nothing will ever happen to you, because I will not allow it."

A single tear streamed her cheek, and she rested her head to his shoulder. "But my father—"

"—Will never again harm you," Jean Marc asserted.

"Oh, no. What have you done?" She flinched and met his stare, as her imagination ran amok. "Despite everything he has done, tell me you did not kill Papa, as I could not live with that stain on my conscience."

"Calm yourself, Maddie." With a cherubic manner that did not fool her for a second, her husband pressed a palm to his chest. "And I am surprised at you, as I have changed. But I met with your father before we cast off from Port Royal, and we enjoyed a civilized conversation, which led to a mutual agreement, the sum of which is that we decided it would be better for all parties involved if he never had anything to do with you again. In fact, as a show of good faith, I promised him and his charming countess that they would not die by my hands, and your father insisted I accept your mother's cameo, which I intended to gift you on your birthday, next month, so you may put your pretty mind at ease."

Framing his face, she emitted a half-sob. "I love you. Have I told you that, today?"

"Ah, my charming society miss, I love you, too." Then he opened the leather portfolio and scanned the documents therein. When his muscles tensed, he peered at her and frowned. "What is this, *Mon Chou*?"

"Exactly what it states." After claiming a quick kiss, she nuzzled his temple. "While you were imprisoned, I did more than summon assistance to support our cause and win your freedom. I ordered the Crawford family solicitor to draw up my will, designating you as sole beneficiary, but I did not stop there. Per my directive, Mr. Parker reissued the deeds to all my holdings, to reflect my new status as your wife and include you. As such, we share joint ownership of the estate."

"You did that for me?" Shuffling her in his

grip, Jean Marc held her at arm's length. "Why?"

"Because what is mine is yours, and I will withhold nothing from you." She assumed a resolute stance. "Not now, not ever."

Without a word, and to her confusion, he set her aside, rose, walked to the water, and dove beneath the surface. Maddie stood and shielded her eyes from the glare of the sunset. Nervous, she advanced but paused when he reappeared.

Approaching, he favored her with his piratical grin. "Hold out your hands, *Mon Chou*."

She did as he bade, and he placed a pile of gold and glittering gemstones in every conceivable color in her clutch. "Jean Marc, where did you get this?"

"That is insignificant." He chuckled. "But I am no pauper, and our babes will never know hunger." He glanced over his shoulder. "There is an underwater cave that lies beneath the ledge, and it is well hidden and loaded with chests filled with similar booty." He tucked a stray tendril behind her ear. "Should anything happen to me, you are to engage Tyne to collect the treasure for our family."

"Do you think it prudent to leave a fortune in gold and jewels secreted in a cave on an abandoned island?" As she assessed the condition of the riches, she gulped and gingerly placed the items in the sack. "If you prefer, we could meet with my banker, when we return to Boston, and arrange to have the items transferred into more secure storage."

"Perhaps that is a good idea." Her husband studied her, and then his dogged composure broke, and he tickled her and growled. "Ah, I love you *Mon, Chou.* I would bath your naked body in a fortune, but nothing compares to the priceless masterpiece I married."

Laughing, they donned their clothes, trading tender caresses and sweet kisses, as they packed the blanket and the ledger in the sack. At last, Jean Marc bent at the waist, as she stood on the rock and perched on his back. With his hands supporting her knees, she wound her arms about his shoulders, and he carried her back to the landing site, where Tyne would take them back to the ship.

As her pirate trudged forth, Maddie suckled and laved his neck, nibbled the crest of his ear, and whispered salacious innuendos intended to entice and arouse her buccaneer. And she counted each flex of his muscles and accompanying grunt and groan as an invaluable boon and a promise.

On the beach, a single torchlight marked the first mate's location, and Jean Marc conveyed her to the jolly boat.

"I will be on my knees, in your bunk, when you arrive, my love," she vowed, as they pulled near the hull of the *Morass*. It dawned on her then that so much had changed since last they ventured to their special place, and she recalled his words of comfort on the afternoon he first claimed her bottom. With a wink and a smile, she teased his healthy erection. "But you may decline at any time, and I will stop."

"You tempt me, *Mon Chou*, and that is never wise." Jean Marc narrowed his stare, but the hint of a grin belied any disquietude. "Whatever am I to do with you?"

"My lusty captain, you are a clever man, and I am certain you will think of something particularly naughty." Wrenching the hair at the nape of his neck, she bit his lip. "And I will enjoy every minute of it."

EPILOGUE

November, 1816

A cold wind signaled an early winter, as Jean Marc stood on the quarterdeck and directed the helmsman, and they glided the ship alongside the *Demetrius*. On the bow, a familiar face lingered, and Lady Elaine waved a greeting, which he mirrored.

"Oh, I am so excited, my love." At his side, Maddie bounced and hugged her round belly. "And I am so proud of you."

"I never could have succeeded without you, *Mon Chou*." He pressed his lips to hers, as the Iron Corsair smirked. "And no snide comments from the gallery."

Barry laughed. "I have to do something, as I cannot believe I am about to embark on the same lunacy you completed."

"You want to go home." Jean Marc shrugged. "It is understandable and necessary, but you never told me how you came to be a pirate."

"I was blamed for a crime I did not commit." Barry shifted, as the crew prepared the mainsail hull. "Are you sure I am doing the right thing?"

"Do you want to spend the rest of your life looking over your shoulder?" Jean Marc descended the companion ladder and lifted Maddie down. "Or do you want something more?"

Ah, something more.

At the mention, his wife glowed, and he winked.

It was a strange emotion—love.

He understood why women existed for it, and why men killed for it. Love made him believe in the goodness of a lady's heart, in the power of a whisper of a kiss, and in the incomparable strength of his wife's faith. Indeed, what he shared with Maddie knew no bounds. A limitless, seemingly infinite depth of devotion invested even the simplest action, and he wondered how he ever survived without her.

"Welcome, Jean Marc and Lady Madalene." Lady Elaine gathered with Sir Ross and Lord Raynesford. "And I see you renamed the ship *Lady Madalene*. How fitting."

"It is wonderful to meet you, at last." Maddie stepped off the plank and straight into Lady Elaine's embrace. And as the women quickly became lost in chatter, Jean Marc shook Sir Ross's hand.

"It is good to see you again, Logan." Then he snickered. "Never thought I would ever say that."

"That goes for both us." Sir Ross gazed at Barry. "And who is this?"

"A friend who would like to avail himself of a pardon." Jean Marc glanced at the Iron Corsair. "He is known as—"

"—Barrington Nicholas Peregrine Howe." Raynesford opened and then closed his mouth. "Or as he was called when we attended Eton together, the Marquess of Ravenwood."

Now that was a surprise Jean Marc did not see coming.

"Raynesford." Barry dipped his chin. "It has been a long time."

The marquess shook his head. "I have not

seen you since—"

"—I was charged with a murder I did not commit," Barry replied. "Will the King's concordat grant immunity from a crime for which I was never tried or convicted?"

"It is a full pardon." Sir Ross shrugged. "I presume so."

"I have no interest in reclaiming the title." Barry gazed at the sky and sighed. "I just want to be free of the past."

"Then sign the document, and your year commences from this date." Ross flagged a crewmember, which brought forth a tray with a pen, an inkwell, and rolled parchments. "Jean Marc, may I present you a full and unconditional pardon, commissioned and sworn by His Majesty."

"But, of course." He scratched his name on the pact.

"So how did a brash, barely-ex pirate win that dainty little thing?" Sir Ross inquired, as he scratched his chin. "Because you strike me as a rather odd couple."

"I have no idea." Jean Marc expelled his breath to dry the ink. "But I could ask the same of you."

"I am equally dumbfounded." Sir Ross chortled, but his expression softened as he gazed on Lady Elaine. "But I am grateful my wife deems me worthy of her heart, and I endeavor to deserve her, every day."

"*Mon 'Ami*, I know just how you feel." With Maddie's dream within reach and newfound hope for a bright future, Jean Marc held the paper, as Sir Ross affixed his signature and a wax seal.

"Perhaps, some day, we might work together to make the world a better place for our children." Then the Englishman presented the entente.

"Sir Ross, I look forward to it." A series of images flashed before Jean Marc, as he accepted the symbol of his liberty. And in that instant, Maddie rushed forward, tears in her blue eyes, and threw her arms about him. When she retreated, she daubed her face with her lace-edged handkerchief, and he adored the contradiction she manifested.

In public, his bride maintained the air of refined elegance that characterized her from the moment they met. But in private, she could best the most seasoned courtesan, and that was a compliment and an unexpected but much appreciated boon. Yet, most important of all, she loved him.

"Lady Elaine has invited us to visit them in London." Maddie turned to Ross's wife. "And you simply must come to Boston and stay as our guests."

"Of course, we will." To his amazement, Lady Elaine rose on tiptoes and pressed a chaste kiss to his cheek. "So it appears you found someone to love you, Jean Marc. Did I not tell you it was possible?"

"Indeed, and you were right. But it appears fate bestowed upon you a similar gift, Lady Elaine. It is safe to presume your husband no longer ignores you, given the evidence of his affection, which precedes you." When the women gasped at his scandalous comment, he winked and peered at her enormous belly. To Ross, Jean Marc said, "If we are done, we should depart for Port Royal, as Maddie wishes to preside over a Thanksgiving feast at Fair Winds, despite the fact that it is an American custom."

"But I am an American, so the location matters not, as long as we are together." His bride canted her head and cast a heated stare that garnered his attention. "And I want us to savor the sights and sounds of the city, as we had so little time to enjoy Port Royal on our maiden voyage."

"I could offer an extended tour of the prison, as I know it well." He joked. "But the wind alters direction, and the weather turns, so we must be on our way, *Mon Chou.*"

"Take care, Jean Marc." Logan again extended a hand in friendship. "If you ever have need of my assistance, have your wife write me a letter, as she excels in it."

"Believe me, she excels at many things." Jean Marc rolled his eyes and handed his bride across the plank. "And you do the same, but remember, if you ever make Lady Elaine cry, you will still answer to me."

When they regained the relative comfort of his ship, Jean Marc hailed Tyne, and the first mate barked a series of commands. The crew scrambled into the ratlines and adjusted the sheets. Soon, the vessel glided south, toward Jamaica.

"I need a drink, as I already regret what I just did, but I suppose it is too late to change my mind." Barry saluted. "Enjoy your triumph, my friend, while I seek comfort in a bottle of rum."

And so the *Lady Madalene*, with a pristine coat of paint, new canvas and lines, and the devil fresh-paid with pitch, soared on the ocean, and Jean Marc held Maddie close on the bow, as they admired the sunset. It was in those quiet moments, when he embraced his wife, heavy with their unborn child, that he realized he had reclaimed that part of him that he thought he lost, when he undertook a yearlong period of service to the Crown.

Indeed, it was not the violence he committed that made him a man or the temperance of such inclinations that exhibited weakness. Rather, it was in the choice to abstain from such brutality that evidenced his inner strength. And it took the determination of a delicate woman, who accepted him, faults and all, with a spirit to match his own to help him recognize that simple truth.

"Did I embarrass you in front of our friends?" He stuck his tongue in his cheek.

"Never, as I adore you." She nuzzled his chest, burrowed beneath his greatcoat, and wrapped her arms about his waist. "So how do you wish to celebrate, as I am most definitely at your service, and I do so cherish your particular brand of ravishment?"

Yes, Maddie was his anchor. And he appreciated the fact that she never tried to change him. It was for that reason he tried hard to be a better man. For a second, he considered her offer, and then he grinned. "I want to take you to our cabin and ride your round bottom until dinner."

Well, perhaps Jean Marc did not change so much.

To wit she burst into laughter. "Oh, my love, you say the sweetest things."

ABOUT THE AUTHOR

Bestselling, Amazon All-Star author Barbara Devlin was born a storyteller, but it was a weeklong vacation to Bethany Beach, DE that forever changed her life. The little house her parents rented had a collection of books by Kathleen Woodiwiss, which exposed Barbara to the world of romance, and Shanna remains a personal favorite. Barbara writes heartfelt historical romances that feature flawed heroes who may know how to seduce a woman but know nothing of marriage. And she prefers feisty but smart heroines who sometimes save the hero, before they find their happily ever after. Barbara earned an MA in English and continued a course of study for a Doctorate in Literature and Rhetoric. She happily considered herself an exceedingly eccentric English professor, until success in Indie publishing lured her into writing, full-time, featuring her fictional knighthood, the Brethren of the Coast.

Connect with Barbara Devlin at BarbaraDevlin.com, where you can sign up for her newsletter, The Knightly News.
Facebook:
https://www.facebook.com/BarbaraDevlinAuthor
Twitter: @barbara_devlin

Printed in Great Britain
by Amazon